Isaac

Isaac

Allee Mead

Space Wizard Science Fantasy
Raleigh, NC
www.spacewizardsciencefantasy.com

Publisher's Note: This is a work of fiction. Names, characters, places, and incidents are a product of the author's imagination. Locales and public names are sometimes used for atmospheric purposes. Any resemblance to actual people, living or dead, or to businesses, companies, events, institutions, or locales is completely coincidental.

Cover Design by MoorBooks
Editing by Courtney Brooks
Book Layout © 2015 BookDesignTemplates.com

Isaac/Allee Mead.— 1st ed.
ISBN 978-1-960247-41-4

To Christopher: the Crow to my Tom Servo.

CONTENTS

Eleanor

Eleanor's fingers twitched above her desk.

The wall panel stood pulsing blue before her, waiting for her to tap her query into the virtual keyboard. When she'd first moved into this house, the sales rep had insisted on the 48-inch panel. "Forty-eight at least," he'd said. "Everyone else is going half-wall or wall-sized. I mean, this is where people watch movies, use their computers..." But she'd haggled him down to the 24-inch. Even this size seemed blinding at times.

She swiped away the search browser. Then tapped it open again. She had spent most of that week asking coworkers if anyone was interested in attending a free concert in the park that Saturday: a cover band of a 90s group one of her dads had loved. She had been filled with excitement when she'd first heard about the event, but that excitement had deflated with each *no* she received. One coworker had replied that the kids had an out-of-town softball tournament. Another said the in-laws were coming over. Camping trip. Family reunion. Painting the nursery.

They were a good group to work with. They were. She ate with them at lunch; they included her on the email chains of inside jokes. They breathed life into a cubicle landscape.

They were just busy.

And most of the time, she didn't need to be social. Most days, she just wanted to be home and surround herself with her books and watch a show on the wall panel. She had convinced herself it'd be enough to just listen to music that night. But Saturday night was here, and she was staring at her browser.

I'm just looking, she reminded herself. *I'm not actually going to buy one…*

"Hi! I'm Gwen," the chat window said. "What can I help you with today?"

Eleanor tried to close the window but accidentally hit the phone icon.

"Shit, shit, shit…"

The call connected before she could close out of it. She could technically still cancel the call, but now she'd be hanging up on someone. She'd forgotten this was a new feature on some sites, where customers could connect directly with a customer service rep. The expertise of a brick-and-mortar employee with the convenience of online shopping. The wave of the future, apparently. She'd heard the company's CEO had originally envisioned video calls, but several employees and a customer focus group said absolutely not.

Gwen repeated her question.

"Hi, Gwen. I'm just browsing."

"Of course. A caregiver robot for you or a loved one?"

"I'm not buying anything today." But Gwen waited for a response. "For me, I guess."

"Of course. May I ask what particular disability or medical condition you have? Or what activities of daily living you need assistance with?"

"Oh, no." Thank God Gwen couldn't see Eleanor's burning face. "I was thinking more for—it's stupid, forget it."

"Ma'am, the bots are for everybody. It's not stupid at all!"

"Okay." But the burning crept down her neck and chest. "I, uh, was thinking of one for"— What was the word she wanted?—"companionship, I guess."

Now it was Gwen's turn to get uncomfortable. "Oh. Ma'am, I'm afraid we don't sell sex robots."

"No! No-no-no-no-no-no-no-no-no. Not a *Firefly* companion, a *Doctor Who* companion. Like, someone to go to movies and concerts with."

Gwen's silence reminded Eleanor that not everyone knew the TV shows Dad loved to watch. "Never mind. Like I said, I was just browsing." She swiped the window closed and powered down the wall panel.

"Stupid," she muttered.

* * *

A ringing startled Eleanor awake the next morning.

She rolled over and fumbled for her watch on the nightstand. Her sister's profile picture glowed back at her. She answered the call without lifting her head off the pillow.

"Yeah?" Her voice was thick and barely audible.

"Oh, shit, it's only six o'clock there. You want me to call back?"

"No, s'fine, Cass." She dug the heel of her hand across her eye, trying to wipe away the sleep. "What do you want?"

Silence. Just long enough to make Eleanor wonder if she had already said something wrong.

"Nor, Dad died."

Eleanor sat up. "Oh."

"Thought you should know."

"Yeah, of course—"

"I have to work through Wednesday, and I'll have to leave Sunday already," Cass said. "But I can drive up to you Saturday if you want to grab dinner or anything."

"I'll see you at the funeral, won't I?"

"Oh. Okay. I didn't know if you wanted to come—"

"Of course I'm coming," Eleanor said.

"Well, I didn't know."

Eleanor pinched the bridge of her nose. *Don't fight with her, please don't fight with her...* "What do you want me to help with? I can drive home today and start planning or sorting through stuff."

"Yeah. Call Mr. Salo or whoever the funeral director is now and see if we can plan for a Friday morning service. Let me know when you're meeting with him and I can video-call in."

"Will do."

"I gotta get going."

"Okay. Safe travels, Cass."

"Yep. Bye."

* * *

Eleanor's rental van left the highway and crunched along the gravel road. Thanks to the van's autopilot, she had spent the five-hour drive across North Dakota writing a to-do list in her notebook. Her other father, Papi, had passed away when she was fourteen, but Dad had planned that funeral. Eleanor had no experience with this.

Their home poked its green roof over the sloping hill. She pulled up the driveway and stopped before the garage. The place didn't look any different from when she'd lived there last. Clean yard and siding. Meticulous garden. Whoever Cass hired to take care of Dad must've done this, or Cass had hired a gardener too; there was no way Dad could've completed yardwork in his condition.

She approached the front porch and tapped 5263 into the digi-lock. Denied. She tried 7849. Denied. She only had one more try before the alarm system called the police.

"Text Cass," she told her watch. "What's the passcode? I tried 'LANE' and 'RUIZ' but no luck. Send."

The door clicked and swung open.

"Text Cass. Never mind, I got it. Send."

Delayed reaction, she guessed. Maybe the digi-lock was breaking down and needed fixing. She'd have to let the real estate agent know. She pulled the notebook out of her pocket and added "digi-lock" and "real estate agent" to the list.

She stepped inside and took off her sandals in the entryway.

"Eleanor."

She jumped at the noise. Her name was said pleasantly, but she didn't recognize the voice.

Without moving or making a noise—besides her thumping heart—she looked around but couldn't see anyone. She peered into the office. Cass's softball bat was probably in the garage, along with hockey sticks and anything else she could swing at the intruder.

She settled for a thick book from the entryway bookcase. The scar on her left arm twinged as she slowly moved forward.

The air conditioning kicked on, causing her to yelp and drop the book.

"Are you okay?"

There was a man on the threshold between her dads' bedroom and the living room. He was dressed in dark grey jeans and a light blue sweater. His hands were empty. "I'm sorry the house isn't clean. I was asleep. Would you like something to eat?" He walked toward the kitchen.

"Who are you?"

"Isaac." He opened the freezer and pulled out a glass container of leftovers.

With his back to her, Eleanor threw up her hands in frustration. *Stay calm. You don't know why he's here or what he wants.* "What are you doing here?" She tried to keep her voice level.

"I'm making lunch." He pulled one plate out of the cupboard.

"No, I meant—" She took a steadying breath.

He put the container in the microwave. Without his pressing a button or giving a voice command, the microwave whirred to life.

Eleanor's face fell. The door unlocking with no one there, Isaac already knowing her name...

"Would you like something to drink?" He turned to her.

She stared at him.

"Water? Milk? Pop?"

She glanced back at her dads' bedroom. "Um, could you get me an orange soda? I think there's some in the garage fridge."

He nodded and left the kitchen. When he crossed a certain part of the hallway, she looked away before the memory could resurface.

She waited until she heard the door click shut before she moved toward her dads' bedroom. Inside, she glanced around. Nothing out of the ordinary. Then in the bathroom she spotted it: a white monolith of a device, with a wider top and base.

A charger.

"You're a care-bot," she gasped.

"There's no orange soda in the garage," Isaac said, now standing next to her.

Eleanor jumped, clutching her heart.

"I startled you again. I'm sorry. Would you like milk or water to drink?"

She glanced at him, then at the charger. "I, uh, didn't know Dad had a care-bot."

"Yes, Cassandra purchased me five years ago when Johnathan could no longer live alone safely." The microwave dinged. "Lunch is ready."

He left the bathroom and Eleanor stared after him.

In the dining room, Eleanor found a chicken salad sandwich waiting for her. Isaac stood attentively, his hands clasped in front of him. Was he really going to stand there like that the whole time?

She took a bite and grimaced.

"Is it not to your liking?"

"It's just—chicken salad doesn't freeze well, not when you've already mixed in the mayo. It doesn't microwave well, either."

"My apologies. When I first arrived here, Cassandra had asked me to freeze the leftovers. I didn't realize the flavor would change. I'll make you something else."

"No, I'll get it."

She found another container in the freezer labeled *penne rosa*. She glanced at the microwave. Isaac must be connected to the smart appliances and the digi-lock. She popped the container into the microwave and pressed the buttons.

Eleanor's wrist buzzed with a text from Cass: *The passcode was 2277 when I was home last.*

2277. CASS. She must've changed it after Eleanor had moved out.

"Do you want to sit with me?" she asked Isaac, who was now standing attentively next to the pantry.

He nodded and took a seat in the dining room.

The microwave dinged, and she joined Isaac at the table. She paused mid-bite when she caught his eyes on her. "Could you not watch me eat, please?"

"Would you like me to face the wall?" he asked sincerely.

"No, just less eye contact. If that's okay."

He nodded and looked down as if in prayer.

"This is really good, by the way."

"Can I look up to talk to you?"

"Yeah, of course."

His head popped up. "Thank you. I'm glad you're enjoying it."

"This is one of Dad's recipes."

"Yes. Cassandra uploaded his and Javier's recipes."

"Can you only make those, then?"

"No, I can look up other recipes as requested. But as Johnathan's condition progressed, I thought it best to stick with familiar foods. Eventually he stopped eating, of course, when his body forgot how to swallow."

The bite of pasta soured in her mouth. She changed the subject.

"How did you know who I was?"

"Cassandra uploaded me with photos and tagged the people in them. It's a multi-purpose feature for care-bots, a security feature for the digi-lock and a photo album I can cast to the wall panel. She also uploaded his favorite music, which can be beneficial for dementia patients. Would you like to listen to anything while you eat?"

For a wild moment, Eleanor pictured him tilting his head back and opening his mouth like a Victrola. Then she realized he could probably just operate the speakers in the house the same way he opened the door. "No, thank you." She raised her glass of milk and quickly realized it had spoiled. She set it down. "You said you were asleep earlier?"

"Yes. When Johnathan died early this morning, I alerted the funeral home and Cassandra, his emergency contact. After his body was taken, I switched into sleep mode. This recharges me and shuts me off until another human is detected at the house."

He nodded in her direction. She didn't say anything. He was so factual, conversational even, about Dad's death, like he was giving her a museum tour.

"Are you finished?"

She nodded. He picked up the dishes and brought them into the kitchen.

Eleanor grabbed her suitcase from the entryway and started upstairs. The memories began seeping in, replaying the last time she was here.

Dad had been diagnosed the summer after Eleanor's high school graduation. When they came home from the doctor's appointment, Eleanor contacted the college she'd been accepted to and withdrew. She got a job at the grocery store, while Cass picked up a few hours every week as a server in the nursing home's dining area. After Cass graduated high school, Cass started working as a certified nursing assistant.

One day, about six years after Dad's diagnosis, Eleanor had been making lunch and spilled pasta sauce on her shirt. She had run upstairs to change and had come downstairs to find Dad in the kitchen holding the knife Eleanor had been using to slice zucchini. He wasn't holding the knife threateningly, just casually, like he didn't even know it was in his hand. That wasn't any more comforting to Eleanor.

"Dad, give me the knife, please," she said, trying to sound gentle.

He didn't seem to hear her. He just walked toward the door leading to the garage.

"Dad..."

She approached him and touched his shoulder as gently as she could. She still startled him.

"It's okay, I just need that back," she said.

"No."

"Dad, please."

"No!"

He was going to hurt himself if he kept moving around. She took his wrist because she didn't want to grab the blade. But he hated being touched.

"No!"

"Dad—"

She gasped as his wrist twisted against hers. Her forearm splashed red as the knife clattered to the floor. Dad started to lose his balance. Eleanor grabbed his arms to steady him, but he hated that too.

"No! No! No!"

"I'm just trying to help, you little shit." It had just slipped out.

The door to the garage opened. Cass stood, her arms full of groceries, taking in the sight before her.

"What did you do?" Cass yelled over Dad's shouting.

"What did *I* do?" Eleanor yelled back, clapping a hand over the bleeding.

Cass set the groceries down and tended to John while Eleanor whipped the dish rag off the oven door handle and wrapped it around the cut. She grabbed the knife off the floor and put it in the sink, then took another dish rag and made a quick pass with it across the floor before dropping that in the sink too. Then she turned off the stove burner and moved the saucepan, the sauce inside angrily bubbling and hissing.

The shouting had stopped. Cass was talking quietly to Dad in that voice she had perfected at the nursing home. Even when she was stressed, Cass seemed to have a well of patience that Eleanor could never tap.

Eleanor wedged herself between the wall and the two of them, then past the groceries in the hallway.

"Where are you going?" Cass asked.

"Hospital," Eleanor snapped.

In the car, everything finally quieted down as it drove her to the hospital. Now she could really feel the throbbing stinging of the cut. She shook and cried and swore the whole ride there.

The doctors stitched her up and sent her home. She stepped inside the house, the hallway now clear of groceries and the floor clean once again. Dad's music flowed softly from the wall panel in the living room, where Dad and Cass were sitting.

Cass looked at her. Eleanor glanced away, only lifting her left arm to show her sister the bandage. Her stomach roiled. The two of them didn't talk until after they had put Dad to bed. They went upstairs and sat on the couch.

"Does it hurt?" Cass asked, keeping her voice low.

Eleanor nodded.

"We just have to wash and put away knives when we're done with them. Dad won't grab one if he can't see it."

"We need to put him in a nursing home. Do you get any sort of discount at work?"

"Eleanor—"

"Well, we clearly can't take care of him."

"You had one accident. It won't happen again if we just hide the knives."

"Cass—"

"He's going to get worse in a home. It's a completely unfamiliar environment to him, even with me there."

"He's not going to get better here."

"I know he's not going to get better," Cass snapped. "But he'll be less agitated here."

Eleanor held up her bandaged arm. "*This* is less agitated?"

"Let's just hold off on the nursing home, okay? I'll tap into more resources at work. With more support, we can still do this."

"Do whatever you want." Eleanor stood up.

"The fuck is that supposed to mean?"

Eleanor threw her arms up in defeat as she walked into the bedroom they still shared.

She stayed in town long enough to help Cass hire a part-time caregiver and to line up a new job and apartment for herself. She should've picked a community that was closer, but she didn't. Some part of her couldn't. She rented a moving van and made the five-hour drive from Hazen to Grand Forks. Every paycheck she tried to squirrel away some money for a house—she quickly learned how much she hated sharing walls with strangers—and sent some money back home.

Cass accepted the money but never sent a reply. A year later, Cass called to say she had found a full-time caregiver for Dad and was moving overseas. Slowly Cass reached out more and more—mostly on holidays and birthdays, including Javi's—but they never bridged that gulf between them.

Javi

Javi held the tumbler of coffee to his forehead and closed his eyes. He couldn't feel any heat through it like he could with his mugs at home, but he hoped the pressure would calm him. Twenty minutes. Twenty minutes of peace before he had to leave the park and go back to work.

So, of course, the silence was interrupted by a man around his age with two kids. The man collapsed onto a bench two picnic tables away; he had a 10-month-old baby strapped to his chest and a four-year-old pulling at her ear and whining.

"Yeah, one second, Eleanor."

The four-year-old grew louder.

"I'm looking," the man said, gently enough but clearly overwhelmed. He pawed through the giant baby bag. He found a sippy cup, but the lid came loose and the contents cannonballed the sidewalk. "*Shit. Shit.*"

Javi allowed himself one eyeroll before picking up his lunch bag and tumbler and striding over. "It sounds like she has an ear infection."

The man was using a bib to mop up the juice and didn't look up.

"I'm a pediatrician. If you want to follow me to the clinic, I'll take a look."

The man looked up, the skin under his eyes a deep purple. Javi could almost see the man's brain register his words in real time. The man nodded. Javi shouldered the baby bag and led the family to his office next door.

"Eleanor," Javi said, "do you want help getting on the exam table?"

She shook her head and climbed up. She spotted the picture frame on Javi's desk and gave an excited gasp.

He grabbed the frame and handed it to her. "You want to look at my dogs while I look at your ear?"

She pored over the photo as if it were a sacred text.

"What's this one's name?" She pointed at one.

"Joey."

"What's this one's name?"

"Justin."

"What's this one's name?"

"Lance."

"Where are JC and Chris?"

Javi glanced at the man, impressed, then back at Eleanor. "The shelter said I couldn't take five at once, so that's what I'll name my next two dogs."

"Daddy doesn't like NSYNC."

"Oh, he prefers Backstreet Boys?"

"No. My Chemical Romance."

Javi glared at him. "I should write you up for that." Then he saw Eleanor's worried face. "I'm just teasing him. He didn't do anything wrong. Anyway, middle ear infection." He turned to the man. "How long has she been fussing like this?"

"Uh..." He stared off into space, his mouth hanging open. "Couple days, maybe?"

"I'll prescribe amoxicillin, then. When was her last check-up?"

"I brought them both in a couple weeks ago."

"Who did you meet with?"

The man shook his head. He was on the verge of tears. "I don't remember."

"You in our system?"

"Yeah. John. Johnathan Lane."

Javi typed away at his computer. "Oh, with Dr. Carlton. *And* you were his last appointment of the day, meaning he spent maybe five minutes with you before rushing off to his tee time. Yeah, he's trash. I'm switching you over to my patient list and we're doing that appointment over. Looks like Eleanor's only had that one appointment with us."

"Yeah, they only moved in with me about a month ago." When Javi gave him a confused look, he continued. "I fostered for twenty years. Teenagers, though, so I'm still learning how to do all of this. I used to foster Eleanor's and Cassandra's mom. She reached out to me, saying she couldn't take care of them anymore, so I'm in the process of adopting them."

"That's incredible," Javi said breathlessly. He gazed at John a little too long. He cleared his throat. "Let's do that check-up."

Javi examined Eleanor while John unbuckled Cassandra from the baby carrier. Javi helped Eleanor off the table and took the baby. He watched John's eyes land on Javi's lunch bag and tumbler.

"This was your lunch hour. I took up your free time."

"Hey, that's no problem," Javi said. "It's an appointment now anyway, so surprise!"

"I'm sorry. I mean, thank you, but sorry. And thank you. If there's anything I can…" John's voice trailed off, like his thinking had run out of minutes.

Javi examined Cassandra then handed her back to John, who wrangled her back into the baby carrier. Javi pulled a prescription pad from a desk drawer. Everything had been electronic for years, but he kept one pad for dramatic moments.

"Cassandra's good to go, and you can pick up Eleanor's prescription on your way out. But I'm writing something for you." He jotted it down, ripped the sheet off, and handed it to John, who squinted at the word.

"What are hilachas?" He almost pronounced it correctly.

"My specialty. That prescription is good for one dinner by yours truly. You'll want to take it in the evening."

John stared at the paper, like the words were out of focus. Was he that stupid or that tired? Or that weirded out by a stranger in the park billing him, then hitting on him? Javi might not have thought this through.

"You're the one who gave up your lunch hour. Why are you bringing me food?" He didn't say it suspiciously; he sounded genuinely confused.

"I would like to bring you a meal so you get one night off from cooking and washing dishes. And you'll get some adult company." He hoped he said *adult* in a normal voice. "If that's okay. And not inappropriate."

"Oh. Yeah, that sounds wonderful," John breathed. His face lit up, like a sun breaking through the clouds. "Um, Friday. No, you're probably working Friday. You don't need to work and then cook. Saturday?"

"Saturday works. Six o'clock."

"Yeah, Saturday." John picked up the baby bag and took Eleanor's hand. They left the exam room. John poked his head back in. "You need my address. No, you don't. It's in the system." He poked his head back out.

"Do you want my name?" Javi called, the corner of his mouth twitching into a smile.

John poked his head back in. "Oh, yeah. Sorry. What's your name?"

"Dr. Javier Isaac Ruiz de la Rosa." It was too long of a name for John's tired brain to register. "Or Javi."

"Javi." (Javi's heart thrilled at the sound.) "Saturday. I won't forget." John's head disappeared around the doorframe again.

Javi sat there. He couldn't stop grinning. "He's going to forget," he told the empty room.

Eleanor

Eleanor and Isaac were the first attendees to arrive at the funeral home. Cass had flown in last night and stayed in Bismarck, so she would drive down this morning. Mr. Salo and his assistant gave their condolences then excused themselves so they could finish setting up. Eleanor and Isaac stood there in silence, Isaac comfortably, Eleanor not so much.

"Nor..."

Eleanor turned around. "Hey, Cass."

Cass had on a fitted dress and heels, with a shimmery headband over her twist outs. The two sisters stood for a moment, then pulled each other into a hug. One funeral couldn't melt away six years of tension, but Eleanor could feel a bit of thawing between them. She'd never say it out loud—the thought alone knocked the air out of her lungs—but Dad's death meant one less thing to fight about.

She spotted a guy Cass's age standing behind her.

"Oh," Cass said and started to sign while she spoke, "Eleanor, this is my boyfriend, Abir. Abir, this is my sister, Eleanor, and Dad's care-bot, Isaac."

Had Cass mentioned a boyfriend? She must have. Maybe she didn't. Eleanor thought she remembered a passing comment about an American roommate when Cass had called to say she had taken a job in London. This must be him.

"It's nice to meet you," he signed.

Eleanor had grown up taking ASL classes but hadn't used her skills much since high school. She waved then remembered to bring her hand to her temple and salute.

Abir smiled.

"Abir's glasses translate spoken English into ASL," Cass said. "Just in case you forget a word."

"Oh, that's cool," Eleanor said.

He signed something back, but Eleanor only caught half of it. She turned to Cass.

"He said they give him a headache if he wears them too long."

Eleanor signed "I'm sorry."

"So just try to sign as much as you can," Cass said, while signing so that Abir could see.

"I know you'll be hearing this a lot today," Abir signed, more slowly this time, but Cass still translated, "but I'm sorry about your dad."

"Thank you."

Funeral attendees started to file in.

"Oh, here come the old biddies."

"Cass!"

"What? That's what they call themselves. They have sweatshirts and everything. Started that about a year ago, when Ji-soo turned 70."

"How do you know that?"

"Because I stay in touch with people, Eleanor."

Thankfully, the group of older women weren't wearing their sweatshirts today. They fronted the condolences line, shaking the sisters' hands and feeling sorry for their loss. Ji-soo, Papi's friend and basically an aunt to the girls, pulled Eleanor and Cass in for one of those hugs that seemed to squeeze your soul back into your body.

Mr. Salo filed everyone into pews, and the funeral began. Eleanor listened to the sermon as best she could, but her focus flitted in and out. As soon as Cass started crying, Eleanor had reached for her hand, only to find Abir already squeezing Cass's other one. Did she need two people comforting her?

She could feel Isaac watching her, seeing if she needed comforting too. As his hand moved, she lifted hers and tucked her hair behind her ear. She shook her head at him as imperceptibly as she could.

She felt Cass's eyes on her and stared straight ahead.

When her attention wandered again, she glanced around the funeral home. The place had maybe half the people of Papi's funeral, but he had always been the more social one. Even the people here today were mostly connected to Papi, like his now-retired coworkers who still lived in the area and the family members who had been able to fly in. There were some faces Eleanor didn't recognize, but she didn't know if they were former students or former foster kids. Or maybe they were here for Cass.

I'm going to die alone.

The thought must've been in her head the whole service, swimming below, but it broke the surface during the special music: a Cass-arranged instrumental of "How's It Going to Be."

Dad had a husband and two children and even he died alone. What did Eleanor have? Two dead parents, coworkers she never saw outside the office, a sister across the ocean, an extended family who lived on the coasts. She didn't even have a dog...

Her breath grew shallower and shallower until she couldn't catch it. It even squeaked a bit.

"Are you all right?" Isaac asked quietly. "Would you like to leave?"

God, why did they have to seat family in the front? She'd have to walk past everyone.

She remembered the side door that led to the luncheon area. Still visible to everyone but she wouldn't have to look at them.

She nodded, got up, and fast-walked to the door. She could only imagine how many pairs of eyes were on her as she pulled and pulled at a door that apparently needed to be pushed. She pushed then disappeared from the room.

Isaac followed her. "Do you need to go to the hospital?"

Eleanor shook her head. She sat down, leaning against the wall. Isaac knelt beside her. He took her wrist in one hand and held his other hand inches from her chest. The caterers setting up lunch left them alone.

"Elevated heart rate. Shortness of breath. You're hyperventilating." It was the same voice he used to ask what she wanted for lunch. "Breathe in through your nose and out through your mouth."

He moved his hands away, but she gripped both of them tightly. His skin was rubbery, not completely inhuman but a little unsettling. Heat poured from them like an old, whirring laptop.

He sat with her until her breathing slowed down to normal. She didn't let go of him.

"Do you feel better?"

She nodded.

"Do you want to talk about it?"

She shook her head, but the words gushed out anyway. "He died alone. Papi's gone, Cass and I weren't there..."

"He wasn't alone," Isaac said. "I was with him."

Eleanor stared at him. Her heart rate threatened to elevate again. Another thought was trying to emerge, but she couldn't see it in the murky waters.

The door opened and Cass appeared. Eleanor wrenched her hands out of Isaac's. Cass studied them both.

"Everything okay in here?" she asked, eyebrow raised. "You ready to eat?"

"Yeah," Eleanor said quietly.

Isaac stood and held his hands out to help her up, but Eleanor ignored him and slid up the wall. They followed Cass over to the food just as the other funeralgoers were pouring into the room's main entrance.

Eleanor tucked into the dry sandwiches and watered-down lemonade. She sat next to Cass at a long table with their aunt, uncles, and cousins. Papi's siblings shared stories of Papi and Dad, but Eleanor's mind was still on the floor by the wall. Her eyes drifted over to Isaac, who was handing out drinks at the refreshments table.

Some of the old biddies sat on her other side.

"So, Eleanor," Ms. Henriksen asked, "you have a boyfriend?"

Really, you're asking me at a funeral? Eleanor wanted to scream. "No."

"Girlfriend?"

"No."

"Then who's the snack?" asked Ms. Bad Hawk, jerking her thumb toward the table where Isaac was pouring Abir a glass of water.

"That's Dad's caregiver," Eleanor said as neutrally as she could.

"I've met Isaac. I meant the other one."

"Oh, that's my boyfriend, Abir," Cass said.

"He's cute," Ms. Henriksen said. "You're working in England now, right?"

"Yes, been there five years now."

Eleanor avoided Cass's eyes.

Javi

He definitely forgot. Javi found the house in the country easily enough, but he stood at the door for a few minutes after ringing the doorbell. John answered wearing sweatpants and a vomited-on T-shirt and bouncing an agitated Cassandra on his hip. John stared for a moment.

"Javi," Javi reminded him.

"Javi," John said quickly. He closed his eyes and scrunched his face in apology. "I knew I had something going on tonight. I'm so sorry."

"Do you want to cancel?"

"No, come on in." He opened the door wider and walked away. He came back. "That sounded resigned. Come on in!"

Javi glanced around the entryway and through the open door of the office. The place looked like a college student's: furniture that had been accumulated, not curated; functional pieces working overtime; a few photographs on the wall but no art. No sense of style.

The living room was absolute chaos. John must've hit up some thrift stores, because there were dated toys everywhere. Not an electronic one in the bunch. Eleanor was on the floor playing with some stuffed animals. Javi could hear a tea kettle screaming in the kitchen.

"We'll want to heat up the food first." Javi let himself into the kitchen to set the food down and turn off the stove burner. "Eleanor, how's your ear?"

"Good."

"Doesn't hurt anymore?" He walked back to the living room.

"No." She scanned the area around his feet. "You didn't bring your dogs?"

Javi laughed. "No, the dogs stayed home tonight."

"Oh." Eleanor turned back to her toys.

"But I brought pictures." He handed her a digital frame he had grabbed from home.

He turned to John and reached for Cassandra. "I got her. You go change."

John nodded, still a bit dazed, and headed upstairs.

After Javi one-handedly heated up the food and set the table, John returned in jeans and an ill-fitting button-down. He had somehow missed two buttons while getting dressed. John dished up some food for Cassandra and sat her in her highchair. Javi went into the living room to get Eleanor, her eyes still glued to the frame. He sat her down and cut up her beef, potatoes, and carrots. Then he began to feed Cassandra.

"Oh, you don't have to—" John began.

"Nope. You're eating like an adult tonight."

"Thank you," John said quietly, his voice out of shape.

"How old are your dogs?" Eleanor asked.

"Joey is two, Justin is five, and Lance is nine."

"Do they have toys?"

"So many toys! Stuffed animals, balls, rope toys. Justin is gentle with his stuffed animals, but Lance and Joey like to chew theirs up."

"Where do they sleep?"

"Eleanor..." John said gently.

"She's fine," Javi said to John. "You and I can talk later."

John took a bite of food and moaned, clapping a hand over his mouth. Javi raised an eyebrow and fought back a laugh.

John turned a splotchy red. "Sorry. It's really good and I can't remember the last time I ate something that was still warm."

Javi grinned.

After dinner, John said to the girls, "All right, playtime, story time, bedtime."

Javi stood up. "I'll do the dishes. Do you want the leftovers?"

"Yes, please," said Eleanor.

"You've already done enough," John said.

"Fight me. Go play with your kids."

After what sounded like Eleanor reenacting *Lilo and Stitch* with the stuffed animals, John fed Cassandra a bottle, then took the girls upstairs. Javi snooped through the overstuffed bookcase in the entryway while he waited.

"I *would* pick a sci-fi nerd," he muttered.

He heard footsteps thumping down the stairs.

"You ready for some grownup conversation?" Javi asked.

"Yeah." John rubbed the back of his neck and glanced up the stairs. "Do you want to sit outside? I'll get us something to drink."

Javi stepped outside and sat on the porch swing. He could hear crickets chirping and even spotted some deer in the field beyond the gravel road.

"All I'm missing is a banjo."

John came outside and handed him a mug.

Javi laughed. "Gee, I hope you didn't make me anything too strong."

"Oh, don't worry," John said in all seriousness. "It's decaf."

Javi laughed. He took a sip then grimaced; he hated tea.

"Oh, shoot, you probably drink coffee," John said. "I'm sorry."

"It's fine," Javi said. "So what's on your mind that we need to speak outside?"

"I just—" John sighed. "I just really need to vent, and I don't want to be anywhere where Eleanor can overhear me. I don't ever want her to think I don't want her."

Javi softened. "Of course."

"You're the first adult I've really talked to in a month," John said, his voice like a deflating balloon. "I love them and I don't regret for a moment taking them in, but...I'm drowning. I'm not sleeping, I haven't eaten a meal by myself, I spend every quiet moment freaking out about how badly I could screw this up. Not that I didn't freak out when I fostered, but my house was just a bandage for those kids until their parents were in a better position. But now?" He glanced at the porch ceiling. "I'm the only one who can screw this up."

"What do you have for a support system?" Javi asked.

John shook his head. "No family. The foster kids who stayed in touch don't live close enough to help. I haven't even met with my therapist since the girls came here." He sighed. "How are you so good with kids?" he asked, out of breath.

"I don't have to live with them. I only get them for short spurts."

"Sure, but…When I fostered, teenagers could just tell me what they needed. I mean, I needed to model those communication skills sometimes, but they could just tell me when they were hungry or hurt or stressed. But with Eleanor and Cassandra, I just…It's guesswork. I mean, Jesus Christ, Eleanor had an ear infection for two days and it didn't even cross my mind to take her in."

"Hey, parents make mistakes. They feel guilty. You learn from it and you—"

"No, you want to know how stupid I am? I just walked Eleanor into preschool last week like she'd be fine. And I wasn't even out of the building before they called me back, she was screaming so loud. And Cassandra is on a waitlist for daycare, so I'm trying to be a school counselor with two small kids in my office and I just can't—"

"John." Javi set down his mug and pressed a hand on top of John's, like he was trying to steady a wobbling plate. "You didn't know—"

"I should've eased her into preschool, set up meetings with the teacher—"

"You didn't know. These kids came into your life suddenly. You didn't have time to prepare."

John's breath shuddered. He set his mug on the floor and wiped his eyes with his free hand.

"Call the teacher on Monday," Javi said. "When Cassandra starts daycare, call your therapist. Schedule appointments during lunch if you have to. Join the clinic's parent support group so you can meet new people. You can't take care of the girls unless you take care of yourself."

The porch swing creaked in the breeze. John slipped his hand out of Javi's, picked up his mug again, and finished his tea in silence. Javi picked up his own mug and held onto the warmth.

"I should let you get going," John said.

Javi nodded and stood; he hadn't been in North Dakota long, but he had lived here long enough to know that was how some people ended a conversation. They walked back to the door. John put his hand on the door handle, turned toward Javi, and opened his mouth, like he wanted to ask him something. He closed his mouth and turned away.

"Can I come back next Saturday?" Javi asked.

"No, I couldn't impose." But the relief in his eyes told Javi this was exactly what John wanted to ask.

"You kidding? I love showing off my cooking skills. You haven't even tried my caldo de res, my güicoyitos rellenos..."

John started quoting Kenan Thompson's David Ortiz impression: "Mofongo..."

"Bistec con más bistec..."

John laughed. It was the most relaxed Javi had seen him. "Thank you," he said. "For all of this."

Javi smiled. "I got you."

Eleanor

As they filed out of the funeral home, Eleanor asked Abir if he'd mind riding home with Isaac in John's car. Cass raised an eyebrow but led her sister to her rental.

Eleanor cleared her throat. "So does everyone in town know Isaac's a care-bot and I've just been making an idiot of myself? When I met with Mr. Salo this week, I just talked about Isaac like he was a caregiver."

Cass snorted. "No. I only told Abir. It's nobody's business how much money I spent."

"How much did you spend?" Eleanor knew they couldn't have been that affordable, since she didn't know anyone with a care-bot. Even when she went on the company's website last week, she knew it was more of a whim than serious shopping.

Cass shrugged. When she felt Eleanor's eyes still on her, she added, "It was $50,000."

Eleanor stared at her. "Fifty thousand?" she gasped. "You don't have that kind of money."

Cass rolled her eyes: *I know, idiot.* "I took out a loan."

"You shouldn't have done that—"

"It was the only way Dad could keep living at home."

"But now you're paying interest on—"

"I know how loans work," Cass said. "And you are not lecturing me on this, so drop it."

They arrived home, and Cass and Abir went upstairs to take a nap. Isaac got started on making dinner, and Eleanor kept him company, asking him questions about the technology and swatting away the thought buzzing around her head.

After Cass and Abir woke up and they all ate supper, Isaac suggested watching home videos of Dad—"to help with the grieving process," he said—but Cass wanted to watch a television series she and Abir had already started.

Cass and Abir sat on the couch, his head resting on her shoulder, his glasses in his shirt pocket since the show had subtitles. Eleanor sat in the armchair and kept glancing back at Isaac in the kitchen until Cass caught her.

She faced forward. Watched the show. Fiddled with her watch.

"I think I'll go read upstairs," she said, pulling herself out of the chair and heading toward the stairs.

"We can watch something else," Cass said. Eleanor could practically hear the eyeroll.

"I just want to go upstairs," Eleanor snapped.

Upstairs, she pulled a book out of her suitcase and settled on the couch. She couldn't concentrate but didn't dare turn on the wall panel up here.

After a while, she heard footsteps on the stairs. She rolled her eyes. "I said I'm fine up here." She saw it was Isaac. "Hi."

"Hello. Would you like some company?" Isaac asked.

"Sure." She patted the couch. He sat way too close.

"I can remain quiet if you'd like to read."

"No, you're fine. I can't concentrate anyway."

"What were you reading?"

"*The Hitchhiker's Guide to the Galaxy*. It was one of Dad's favorite books. He and Papi even dressed up as Arthur and Ford for Halloween one year." She pointed at one of the photos on the wall.

He nodded. "Do you miss him?"

"I don't want to do this..."

"Talking is a useful part of the grieving process."

"I get that, but I just spent a whole funeral where people were asking me"—She gripped the back of the couch as if it were a shoulder—"'How are you doing?' 'You doing okay, kiddo?' And I don't have a good answer, because I don't feel anything. I feel like I lost Dad years ago and we're just now holding the funeral, so there's just nothing left."

"You sound a little angry."

"Because I'm tired of people asking me to talk about this!" She pinched the bridge of her nose and took a breath. "And I shouldn't get mad at you because you're just trying to help, but I just don't want to talk about this today."

He nodded, and they sat in silence. Eleanor picked up her book again.

"If you're having trouble concentrating, would you like me to read to you?"

Eleanor glanced at the stairs first, but no one was coming up. "Sure." She handed him the book.

He had such a soft, soothing voice...She stretched her legs onto the ottoman and leaned her head against the back of the couch. He read until Eleanor heard footsteps on the stairs. She snatched the book from his hands, muttered good night, and scurried into the guest room.

* * *

The next morning, Cass asked, "Are we sorting through Dad's stuff today?"

"No Abir?" He had gone upstairs after breakfast.

"He's in grad school, so he has homework."

"Oh, what's he studying?"

"History. You can ask him more about it later." Her tone was friendly enough, but there was an undercurrent of criticism.

Eleanor had barely spoken to Abir since meeting him yesterday. He seemed very nice and funny—his fingers flew and his face grew animated when he talked, and he was good about including Eleanor in his and Cass's conversations—but Eleanor had never been good at small talk with people she'd just met. Her brain thumbed through possible topics only to reject all of them: *I can't ask him if he has pets. What if his dog just died?*

But she had something to discuss with Cass, so she thought it best to ignore her comment.

The sisters went into the basement.

"I sorted as much as I could already," Eleanor said. "The stuff I wanted to keep and the stuff I knew we could throw out. Then I figured you could pick out what you wanted and help me with the rest."

"Great, then we can sort into garbage, recycling, and estate sale."

Eleanor stood to the side while Cass peeled open a storage tote. "Papi's concert tees," Eleanor said. "I took the couple I wanted."

"I know a guy who makes quilts with shirts." Cass started pulling out some of the tees.

"I told Dad to sort through those, like, 13 years ago."

"Yeah, well…" Cass closed that tote and opened another one.

Eleanor slid the tote with the remaining tees into the estate sale pile. "Oh," she said, like she hadn't been practicing this conversation all morning, "I rented a van if there's anything you want to keep but don't want to fly back with you. I can just keep it in my basement."

"Oh, that'd be great, thanks." Cass clicked the lid back on and slid it toward Eleanor. "Estate sale."

Eleanor focused on moving the tote, hoping she didn't look like she was avoiding Cass's eyes. "Yeah, like furniture, exercise equipment, Isaac. Books. Anything that'd be too big or heavy."

"Oh, Isaac I'll be able to sell before we leave."

Eleanor's stomach slipped, as did the tote she was trying to stack. "Sell him?"

"Well, yeah. He's not a new model, but he still works perfectly so he should have a decent resale value that I can put against the loan."

Crap, Eleanor had already forgotten about the loan. She scrambled to restack the tote and to find a new tactic.

"Well, if it doesn't work out before you leave, I can take him." No, that wasn't good enough. Cass would find a buyer the moment Eleanor banked on that not happening. "You know what, you can let me worry about finding a buyer, and that's one less thing on your plate."

"Nor, it's going to take, like, two seconds to make a for-sale post."

"Right, but we want to pair him with a good family."

"He's not a litter of puppies, Nor."

"No, I know that. But we still want to find someone who actually needs him, right? Not..." She cast her hand out for the right word. "Sell him for parts." She cringed. She avoided looking at Cass but could still feel her incredulous glare.

"Sell him for parts?"

"I know—"

"He's useless in parts."

"I knew it was stupid as soon as I said it—"

"Even if you did manage to pop off an arm, it can't do anything on its own. You need the whole system."

"I get it, Cass."

"Sell him for parts," Cass muttered to herself.

"My point is," Eleanor said through gritted teeth, "that I can take him so you don't have to worry about it."

Something must've given her away, because Cass's eyes narrowed. "And sell him, right?"

"Mmm-hmm." She made herself look her sister in the eye.

"Not to have as a snack?"

Eleanor's breath caught in her throat. She glanced at the basement stairs, but no one was coming down. "You know I don't like anyone like that."

"And you look at him like he's the last piece of garlic bread."

"Jesus, Cass…"

"What? You don't need him and I need to pay off the loan, so why is this up for debate?"

"I just thought—"

"And what would you even use him for?" Cass's voice grew louder.

Eleanor's face grew warm. "Look, I just want him to go to concerts and stuff with." Cass rolled her eyes and Eleanor stepped forward. "I just think I would leave the house more if I had company, and you always used to get on my case about getting out more."

"With people. Get out more…with people."

"But if I had him, I'd meet more—"

"No, you wouldn't." Cass's voice was like a mousetrap. "You and I both know you wouldn't. You would glue yourself to his side and never talk to anyone, just like when you followed me around at parties."

Eleanor was close to tears. "I just…want…Isaac. Okay? I'll make it up to you."

Cass stared at her. Then she shook her head and cracked open another tote. "You're pathetic."

Was that a yes? Eleanor decided not to press the issue, and the sisters worked in excruciating silence until Isaac opened the basement door and called down.

"Is everyone ready for lunch?"

"Yeah, Eleanor's starving."

"Well, eat up, there's plenty," Isaac said without any slyness.

Eleanor glared at her sister.

* * *

The silence at the table was so uncomfortable it made Eleanor itchy. Cass just ignored her and talked to Abir. Eleanor wanted to ask Abir about his studies but thought the gesture would feel to Cass less like an olive branch and more like the overly friendly conversation before a sales pitch.

After lunch, Isaac started dishes while the others cleared the table. "Cassandra," he said, "I compiled resale values for similar models and can share those with you whenever you like."

Eleanor froze, her hand wrapped around the salt shaker.

Cass gave her a look, then turned to Isaac. "Change of plans. Eleanor's gonna take you home with her, because she doesn't have any friends."

Eleanor held eyes with her sister for a moment, then pushed past her and out the front door. She curled up onto the porch swing and just stared at the grass. Her eyes grew hot.

She heard the door open, and Isaac joined her.

"Cassandra said I'm leaving with you?"

Her chest prickled as she heard the idea said out loud. "Only if you want to."

"Of course, I'm happy to help. Eleanor, I am so sorry. I didn't realize you had a disability or a medical condition that required my services."

"I don't."

"So why—"

"You heard Cass, I don't have any friends," she muttered, then sighed. "I don't know, I just thought I'd do more—see more shows, try more restaurants—if I just had someone to go with, instead of asking ten people at work and all of them being busy."

"You can't complete those activities by yourself?"

"Well, yeah, but I'd feel self-conscious and I don't always feel comfortable going to things at night."

He considered. "Do you feel anxious in social situations?"

"I mean, they're not my favorite..."

"So I would be helping you navigate them." He cracked a plastic smile. "An emotional support robot, then."

Her breath caught in her throat; the corner of her mouth twitched while she glanced away. "Yeah, something like that."

* * *

"Isaac, can you help?"

The morning everyone was leaving, Eleanor thought she'd packed everything she was planning to bring home. Then she remembered Isaac's charger.

"I'm packing travel snacks right now. Do you want to ask Cassandra?"

Not really. "Sure."

Neither sister spoke as they carried the charger to the rental van.

"Is it going to fit?" Cass asked.

They set it down, and Eleanor opened the back doors.

"Probably have to take some stuff out first," Eleanor said, pulling out boxes and totes. She thought about asking if it really was okay to take

Isaac but bit her tongue. She didn't want another eyeroll and a lecture about how she needed to stop begging for approval. Plus, she didn't want Cass to change her mind.

But she needed to say something, didn't she? They hadn't exactly mended any fences since they'd been home.

They loaded Isaac's charger and Eleanor piled the other items back into the van.

She took a deep breath.

Abir showed up and signed that it was time to leave.

"All right." Cass turned to her sister.

"Safe travels," was all Eleanor said. She hesitated just a moment too long before reaching out for a hug, so now it seemed like an afterthought. Abir gave her a hug too.

She watched their car disappear down the hill.

She made another sweep through the house to make sure it was empty of everything she wanted to take with her. Before locking up, she placed her hand on the doorframe. She stared at it, memorized its smooth cherry finish. Then she turned off the light and locked the door behind her.

Isaac held out his hand. Eleanor took it.

"Do you need help carrying anything?" he asked.

"Oh." She dropped his hand as if it had burned her. "Um, sure." She shrugged a tote bag off her shoulder and handed it to him.

Isaac sat in the driver's seat and Eleanor took shotgun. "It's self-driving," she said.

"I know. It'll be easier for me to override the vehicle if it malfunctions."

"That's how Papi died," Eleanor said automatically. She winced. She really didn't want a five-hour counseling session. She didn't want to relive finding out Papi's brakes had failed, and his car had rolled into the ditch. How Dad moved zombie-like through making meals and driving them to school and helping them with homework. How his smile never lost that strain, even when the grief became easier to carry.

"Do you want to—?"

"I really don't."

Isaac nodded. "Okay."

They rode in silence down the gravel road. As they approached the intersecting two-lane highway, Eleanor remembered the cross driven into the ground at the base of the stop sign. Etched into the metal was Papi's name and years of birth and death.

The van slowed to a stop.

Should she take the cross with her? She wasn't coming back here again. There was nothing to bring her back. Both Papi and Dad had been cremated, their ashes now commingled and divided into an urn for each daughter to have. Eleanor's was packed carefully in a box somewhere in the back of the van.

A pickup and a semi drove past on the highway.

She should've asked Cass what to do. She reached for her watch, then hesitated. Cass leaving the cross made Eleanor think it needed to stay. Besides, the van was rolling forward now.

"Are you sure you don't want to talk about—?"

"I'm sure," she said, her voice gentle but her tone firm.

"It's just that you've had a lot of loss in your life—"

"Play Dad's music, please." Her voice was casual, but she avoided his eyes.

"A Long December" started playing.

"Thanks," she said, her voice barely audible.

Javi

That Saturday night became every Saturday night. Javi continued to bring over food and, to Eleanor's delight, started bringing the dogs. He taught her how to approach new dogs and read their body language, and always made sure either he or John were watching when the girls and dogs were together. John bought coffee for him, both regular and decaf. Every time Javi saw him, John looked healthier, like he was actually getting some sleep and therapy sessions in. John smiled more and contributed more to conversations. You couldn't shut him up once he got started on a book or a TV show he loved.

"Oh, hey," Javi asked one night when they were cleaning up the kitchen. "My friend Ji-soo's having a Halloween party next Saturday if you want to come."

John froze mid-fold of a dishcloth. "Oh."

"You don't have to."

"No, that's—" He thought about it and nodded. "Yeah, that's—yeah. I'll have to get a babysitter. But, yeah, that's—yeah. Thanks for the invite. I haven't been to a party since...God, since college."

"Well, I'd say you're overdue. And the theme is 2009—Ji-soo's pretty strict about people sticking to the theme."

* * *

Next Saturday arrived and Javi drove to John's home to pick him up in his new car, one of those fully self-driving models that had finally been deemed safe enough for public use. Before Javi could reach the front door, John stepped onto the porch, giving last-minute instructions over his shoulder to the babysitter.

Javi eyed his costume. "That feels a little more 2005 than 2009. Are you supposed to be someone?"

John glanced down. "I'm Patrick Stump."

"Who?"

John stared, incredulous. "Fall Out Boy? I mean, technically they went on hiatus in 2009, but I'm hoping your friend's fine with it."

"I'm sure she won't notice," Javi said dryly.

"Who are you supposed to be?"

"I'm The Situation."

John shook his head and shrugged. "Is that a wrestler?"

"Is that a...From *Jersey Shore*??"

"Oh. Right. I've heard of it but never watched it." They walked toward Javi's car. "Like you watched it and enjoyed it?"

"I don't like your tone," Javi said.

"You just seem too smart for shows like that."

"And what kind of shows *should* I be watching?"

They climbed into the car, which then crunched down the driveway. Javi had been blasting music over the car's speakers, but almost immediately John reached over and turned down the volume.

"I don't know, I guess I just pictured you watching documentaries or something," John said.

"You think after a long day I go home and take in more information?"

John held up his hands in surrender. "My mistake."

They sat for a moment in silence. Then John jumped back in. "It's just you make fun of my shows all the time and you're sitting at home watching people flip over tables."

"Your shows are so confusing. Too many characters, too many subplots. And nobody should be allowed to die and come back to life that many times."

"Oh, my bad, I forgot about the stellar writing that is throwing a rosé into someone's face."

Javi genuinely couldn't tell if they were teasing each other or arguing.

The car parked itself—John hadn't even said anything about the new vehicle—and John and Javi walked into Ji-soo's house.

"Oh," John said.

"What?"

"I didn't realize there'd be this many people." Javi could barely hear him over the music.

"It's a party, what did you expect?"

"Like 10 or 15 people, not—" He gestured toward the packed house. "I didn't even know Hazen had this many people."

"Come on." Javi clapped a hand on John's shoulder and led him to the kitchen.

He was about halfway through fixing up John's drink when John said, "Oh, no, I don't drink."

"Oh, really?" John had never offered him alcohol when he came over, but Javi had just assumed he didn't like to drink in front of the kids.

"I drank in college, but..." His voice trailed off. Every once in a while John would bring up his childhood or early adult years only to immediately change his mind.

"Yeah, okay, that's fine." Javi set aside the drink for himself and looked through the fridge. "Do you want soda?" He refused to call it pop.

"Uh, sure. Nothing with caffeine."

Javi was learning quickly what kind of partygoer John was. He handed John a can then finished mixing the drink he had already started. Ji-soo (dressed as London Tipton) grabbed Javi's arm and steered him toward the karaoke machine. After their showstopping performance of "She Wolf," Javi scanned the crowd looking for John but couldn't see him.

He finally found him on the back patio, on his phone.

"Okay, just—let me try talking to her. Eleanor, sweetie, I need you to go to bed. No—I know I normally read to you, but Yelena can read to you tonight and I'll read to you tomorrow, okay?"

Javi sat down next to him.

"Because Daddy's still at the party and I need you to go to bed now. If you don't want her to read you a story, then just go to bed, sweetheart. Okay? Go to bed, close your eyes, and I'll come say good night to you when I get home." Javi could hear some wailing through the phone. "Yelena, yeah, I'm so sorry. I'll try to hurry up here." Like he was at a business meeting or something.

John hung up and sighed, burying his face in his hands. He finally noticed Javi. "I'm so sorry, we should've taken separate vehicles. I'll call a ride-share."

"You're leaving?"

John threw up his hands. "I can't exactly stay and enjoy myself, can I?"

"But you just got here! You haven't danced or sung or eaten anything yet."

"Maybe next year," John said, exhausted. He stood up.

Javi got up too. "If you go, you're just teaching her that you'll come running home every time she throws a fit."

John's voice snapped like a dry branch. "You don't have kids."

They both froze. An apology flitted across John's face, but he turned away and walked back into the house, leaving Javi alone on the patio steps.

Eleanor

"Where would you like my charger?" Isaac asked when they finally reached her house and unloaded the rental van.

"Oh, uh, guest room is fine." She set the van to return itself to the rental company.

Guest room was a bit strong. Eleanor mostly used it for storing anything she didn't want sitting in her unfinished basement. The room had a nightstand and a bed, but even Cass had never slept there.

Eleanor and Isaac carried the charger into the guest room. She slid some boxes over and set the charger against the wall.

She stepped back and wrung her hands. He looked at her and smiled. Her insides scattered. Crap, she did not think this through. Now what?

"Do you need anything else in here, or—"

"No, this is all I need," Isaac said. "I'd like to get a layout of the house and take inventory of your food. Then I can start dinner."

He walked through the house. Was she supposed to follow him? No, that'd be weird. She stayed in her room and unpacked her suitcase. Isaac appeared in her doorway.

"I can wash your clothes."

"No, that's fine," Eleanor said. "I got it."

She went downstairs and put in a load of laundry. When she emerged from the basement, he was inspecting her cupboards.

"You don't have much here. Is grilled cheese and tomato soup all right?"

"Yeah, that's fine." She leaned against the doorframe as he worked. She realized she was staring. "Do you need help with anything?" she asked.

"No, thank you."

"Right, I'm just gonna…" Her sentence trailed off and she left the kitchen.

She sat with a book in the living room, but she couldn't focus enough to turn the page. Should she have stayed in there and talked to him? About what? It was hard enough to come up with conversation topics for actual people. It's not like she could ask Isaac about any hobbies.

She stood up and went back into the kitchen.

"I can set the table while you cook."

"There's no need," he said cheerfully.

"No, it gives me something to do."

But it didn't give her anything to talk about. She pulled two plates out of the cupboard then remembered she only needed one. She grabbed a bowl and spoon, then poured herself a glass of milk, still racking her brain for things to say.

Once again, he sat with her as she ate. She got through one sandwich triangle before she attempted conversation.

"Thanks for cooking."

"That's why I'm here."

She wiped her fingers on a napkin. She drank some soup. She glanced at him. He was looking at her, not intensely, but he didn't look away. Did he blink? He must've. He'd probably freak people out if he didn't.

She looked away. "Sorry, I'm not very good with conversation."

"You were able to converse that first meal."

"Well, yeah, there was a robot in the house. I had a lot of questions."

Isaac glanced around.

Eleanor rolled her eyes. "Right, there's still a robot in the house. I just meant the newness of it." She ate another triangle. "Do you blink?"

"Yes, I'm programmed to blink, approximately as often as humans do."

"Gotcha."

"See, you're conversing just fine!"

Eleanor laughed. "This isn't conversing! I can't ask a human if they blink."

"So you just ask them something else, right?"

"Right, but I overthink even the basic questions. Like my brain goes to worst-case scenarios or I worry my question's stupid." She thought about it. "But I guess I don't have to worry about looking stupid in front of you."

He gave that same smile from before.

She finished the rest of her meal in silence, but it didn't weigh as heavy as before.

"Are you done eating?"

She nodded. He took the empty dishes into the kitchen and started washing pans. Eleanor just sat at the dining room table.

Did she shower now or when he was done? Now might be more polite, instead of just up-and-leaving when he left the kitchen. But later would help the evening pass faster and give her time to think of something to do with him.

She *really* hadn't thought this through.

She was on the cusp of making a decision when he finished the dishes and stepped into the room.

"What else would you like help with tonight?"

"I was just about to take a shower—which I don't need help with—then we could watch a movie. If you want. You don't have to. But I'm going to watch a movie and you're welcome to join me. Unless something else sounds better."

"A movie sounds good," Isaac said. "Do I have your permission to connect to the Wi-Fi?"

"Yeah, sure. Do I need to do anything special?"

"Stand on one foot and tug on your ear."

She glanced down at her feet then back at him, unsure.

His smile was wider now. "I'm kidding. Verbal confirmation is enough. Would you like me to move your clothes from the washer to the dryer?"

"Oh, I forgot, I can—"

"I got it." He crossed the kitchen, and Eleanor heard him descend the basement stairs.

Eleanor spent the shower trying to pick a movie. Tonight was normally MST3K night, but she wasn't sure what Isaac would think of the robots in the show. Or would he just recognize them as puppets?

She could ask him. He probably wouldn't have an opinion.

"Is *Mystery Science Theater 3000* okay?" she asked after the shower.

"Cassandra named that as one of Johnathan's favorite shows. And of course it's okay: It's your choice."

Halfway through the episode, he turned to her. Eleanor paused the show. "What time do you normally go to bed?" he asked.

She glanced at her watch. "In about an hour."

"Oh. And you're well rested?"

"Yeah?" Something clicked in her mind. "You're on Dad's schedule, aren't you?"

"Yes, I'd normally be recharging by now."

"Oh, you can charge whenever you want. You don't need to stay up with me."

"It's fine, I have enough battery for another hour." He sat quietly for a moment, then some sort of realization crossed his face. "Are you employed?"

"Yeah, I have work tomorrow."

"What do I need to do for you?" He was on his feet.

"Nothing. I take the bus to work. Normally, I leave here eighty-thirty and get back around five-thirty."

"Do you need me to pack you a lunch?"

"Uh, sure."

He darted toward the kitchen. He poked his head back into the living room, glancing at the paused show on the wall panel. "Oh, you can keep watching without me."

She jerked her head into a nod.

She finished the episode. Isaac handed over her folded laundry—"Oh, you didn't have to do that," she said—and she put away her clothes and got ready for bed. He stood in the hallway, which wasn't really wide enough for both of them to be comfortable. Well, for Eleanor to be comfortable.

"Anything else I can help you with tonight?"

It was hard to breathe this close to him. Eleanor backed into her room. "No, I'm good, thanks." She stood there. "Well, good night."

She gave an awkward little wave and shut the door.

* * *

The next morning, Eleanor shut off the alarm and lay there, eyes closed. She stretched her limbs and lolled her head side to side.

"Quick question."

She flinched so violently she hit her head against the headboard.

Just enough morning light filtered through the curtains for her to see the silhouette of Isaac kneeling next to her bed.

"*What is wrong with you*?"

"I waited until your alarm went off. Is that not—"

"Waited—how long have you been in here?"

"Johnathan used to wake up at six AM."

"*You've been in here for an hour?*"

His eyes widened. "Are you upset—"

"You *do not* come into my room while I'm sleeping."

Isaac considered this, his eyes darting back and forth across the comforter. "What if it's an emergency?"

"*Is* this an emergency?"

"No." The volume of his voice shrank. "You don't have any egg whites or spinach, so I didn't know what to make you for breakfast."

"I'll make my own breakfast."

"Can I make you some tea?" His voice was eggshell-fragile.

"Sure." She couldn't spit the venom out of her voice. But should she, though? He still hadn't left. "Did you wake up Dad like this?"

"I set an alarm, so I didn't wake him up, but I needed to be on hand when he needed help getting out of bed or going to the bathroom."

Eleanor's sprinting heart finally slowed down to its usual pace. "Oh."

"But you don't need that assistance, so I'll step out now."

Eleanor sighed and threw her head back onto the pillow.

She found a steaming cup of tea on the dining room table and Isaac standing attentively in the kitchen.

"You're really going to stand there and watch me?" she asked, dropping bread into the toaster.

"I'll watch what you make for breakfast so I can do it for you tomorrow." He paused. "I should've had you make your tea so I know how you like it."

"I only brew it for a couple minutes and drink it black."

The toast popped up. Without speaking to him, she spread peanut butter on her toast and sliced up a banana.

He followed her to the table. "Would you like to engage in conversation?"

"No."

"Music? If you'd like to sync me up to your watch—"

"Dad's music. Matchbox Twenty."

"If You're Gone" filled the air.

"If you're interested in healthier breakfast options—"

"Shut up, Isaac." Eleanor closed her eyes and pressed the mug of tea to her forehead.

After breakfast, Eleanor went into the bathroom and got ready for work. She walked into her bedroom but stopped in the doorway. She stared at her closet door.

"Did you pick out my clothes for me?" she called out.

"Yes, do you need help getting dressed?"

"*When* did you do this?"

"This morning when you were slee—" He poked his head into the hallway and saw Eleanor's face. "I messed up again, didn't I?"

"Yeah, ya did." She stepped inside her room and shut the door. She opened it again. "I got myself dressed the whole time we were at Dad's."

"Right. I'm still programmed to care for Johnathan. But now that I'm here—"

"I can dress myself."

"Right. Sorry." His voice shrank again.

She huffed and shut her door.

* * *

At work, Eleanor was halfway through copy editing a press release before realizing she was working out of the Completed folder.

She growled and leaned back in her chair, pressing the heels of her palms into her eyes.

What was she thinking? She brought home a care-bot programmed to aid a 78-year-old man, and for what? To cook and clean for her? To take her to the movies? Snuggle with her on the couch? They weren't even a day in and she'd already yelled at him. She was already sick of him following her around like a shadow.

What was she going to tell Cass?

Oh, God, Cass. She was right. Not only did Eleanor not need Isaac, she hadn't even made it a day without remembering why she didn't have roommates.

She'd have to ask Cass to find him a new home. Her stomach sank at the thought.

"You all right, Eleanor?" a coworker asked, poking her head over the cubicle wall. "You look upset about something."

"Huh? Oh, yeah, my...roommate scared me awake this morning."

The coworker cocked her head. "Roommate? Since when?"

"Oh, uh, he's a friend of my sister's. He's going to grad school here, so I said he could stay with me."

"Oh, okay. Hope he's pulling his weight."

A laugh escaped Eleanor. "That's actually why he woke me up this morning. He wanted to make me breakfast."

"Aww!" She leaned in. "Is he cute?"

"No." Eleanor turned back to her work.

It seemed the quickest way to end the conversation.

* * *

Her watch dinged during a staff meeting. It never rang at work. Without looking, she hit Ignore, put her watch on silent mode, and murmured an apology.

Her boss nodded then dimmed the lights so they all could better see the wall panel.

Her watch lit up again.

"Eleanor, if you need to take that—"

"No, I'm sure it's just—" She saw "ISAAC" scroll across the watch face. How was he already programmed into her watch? "I'll make it quick, sorry. *What*?" she hissed as soon as she stepped into the hallway.

"I'm at the grocery store."

"What?"

"I'm at the grocery store, and I realized I'm not connected to your checking account or credit card. If you allow me access to your watch, I can—"

"No. I'm at work, I'm not doing that."

"But I'm in line. How am I to pay for—"

"You don't. You put each item back where you found it and you go home."

"But—"

She ended the call and stormed back to the meeting room. She stopped at the door, rearranged her face into an apologetic smile, and walked in.

"Sorry," she whispered to the room in general.

"Everything all right?" her boss asked.

"Yeah, it was my sister. Urgent question but not an emergency."

Thankfully no one pried further, because that was all she had for a lie.

At the end of the day, Eleanor went home and found Isaac in the kitchen.

"Listen, about earlier..." They had said it at the same time.

Isaac continued. "I'm still operating off Johnathan's protocols, preferences, and habits. I need to delete those so there's room for yours. I am learning."

"No, I know. I've been living by myself for a while now, so I need to get used to someone else here. I'm learning too."

Isaac gave her a smile that flipped her stomach. "We're learning together, then."

Javi

The next Saturday was approaching like a train, and Javi hadn't heard from John since the party. He didn't know if John still wanted him to come over. Javi didn't know if he wanted to come over.

The whole night had been a bust. Not that Javi had expected some *High School Musical*-esque night of karaoke, but he at least wanted the party to hold some potential for romance. He loved being John's friend, but he thought a change of scenery might spark something.

But the night had left a sour taste in his mouth. What even was their friendship? Javi spending all Saturday cooking and then eating dinner at John's place, always John's place? Maybe it was all for the best. Javi's locum tenens contract would be up in a couple months, and he would be moving on soon enough. Then this town would be the same as the other places he'd lived and worked for the last ten years. Everywhere else he made friends easily, got plenty of dates, stayed in touch online. He was good at breezing in and out of places.

His phone rang. It was John.

"Hey."

"Hey."

Silence. Javi tried again. "Hey?"

"Hey. Look, I'm sorry about the other night. For getting after you and bailing on you."

Javi's anger deflated despite himself. "It's all right. I was being pushy."

"No, I—I want to make it up to you. I'll cook for you sometime. We can go to your place, I've never actually seen your apartment. Or we can go out to eat, there aren't that many restaurants in town but—"

"How about you cook for me when I come over this Saturday?" Javi said. It was hard to stay mad at somebody who gave such a flustered geyser of an apology.

"Yeah. Yeah, that sounds good."

"Are you as good of a cook as I am?"

"No, but I've got one dish I really like, so I'll make that."

Javi grinned. "It's a date." He heard what sounded like a phone slipping out of someone's hand and falling to the floor. "But at some point we're going to learn how to leave the house," he said when he could hear John back on the line.

"Yeah, that's—yeah, that's fair. Bye."

"Bye."

Eleanor

She heard it on the bus's radio: "And don't forget, this weekend is the annual Summer Fest, complete with food trucks and live music." The DJ rattled off times, dates, and location.

I could go to that.

The thought cut in front of her. She could go—without asking around, without waiting for a response, without ultimately sitting at home and missing the event. The thought skipped through her head as she arrived at work and checked emails and copy edited and sat through a meeting.

And I can wear something cute. Do I have something cute? I don't think I have anything cute.

She went shopping after work. From past experience, Eleanor knew she had a small window to plan and do before she talked herself out of something.

Three screen-machines wheeled toward her. The one that reached her first lit up, and the other two barreled toward the customers walking in behind her.

HI!!!! the screen read. WHAT ARE YOU LOOKING FOR TODAY?

"Browsing," she said, loudly enough so it wouldn't ask her to repeat herself. She always said that unless she was in a hurry and didn't know where to look. She side-stepped the screen and found the dresses section.

And there she found it: a red dress, but the patterned cotton softened the rich color. Too casual for work and too fancy for anything she did in her free time. She brought it to the dressing room, where the metal detector-like machine scanned any items that customers took in. It fit *and* she looked cute.

Is this what confidence felt like?

Just before she reached the checkout kiosk, she spotted an apron in the clearance section: white with red hearts, still there months after Valentine's Day. Cheesy, garish, too much. She grabbed it.

* * *

"Hey, Isaac!"

"Hello, Eleanor," he said without poking his head out of the kitchen. "How was your shopping trip?"

"How—"

She stood in the doorframe and thought she saw his face wince in apology. "When you didn't arrive at your usual time, I used your wall panel to track your watch. Once I saw you were in a store, I shut it off. I'm sorry. With Johnathan, Cassandra went through my settings so I knew what I had permission to do. People with dementia can wander off and get lost, so knowing his location was a top priority. I still don't know your preferences."

"It's okay. We'll figure those out this weekend."

He nodded and turned back to fixing supper. Did he look relieved? How often did she admonish him?

"Speaking of..." She took a deep breath. "There's a Summer Fest I'd like to go to this weekend."

"Would you like me to secure a ticket?"

"No, it's a free event." *Oh, come on, Eleanor, if you can't even get up the nerve to ask him...* "I'd like you to come with me. If you want to come."

"Oh, to navigate social anxiety, like we discussed."

Her budding smile withered. "And it's more fun to go with someone," she muttered. She noticed the flour on his sweater. "Oh, and I got you something."

She showed him her purchase.

"It's an apron," was all he said.

"Yeah. Since you don't change outfits and you can't really wash what you're wearing, you can wear this when you cook and it'll keep your clothes cleaner." She tried to read his expression. "Or not. You don't have to."

"It's a gift?"

"Yeah, just a little something—"

"Then I love it." He ducked down so Eleanor could slip it over his head. She tied it around his waist. She snorted.

"Can I take a picture of you?"

He nodded.

She double-tapped her watch and made an L with her finger and thumb to adjust the holo-lens. He tucked his hands into his pockets and gave a practiced smile.

"Click. And now a silly one."

His smile widened and he jutted out his hip.

She laughed, took another photo, and sent it to Cass. Only after she sent it did she realize Cass might be asleep already.

But during dinner, her wrist buzzed with a text: *You kiss the cook yet?*

Eleanor typed back: *Why are you like this.*

* * *

The day of the Fest, she groaned at her reflection. She had thought braids would look cute with this dress, but she looked like a child.

"Is there something I can help you with?" Isaac stood in the bathroom doorframe.

"How are you with hair?"

In the living room, while she sat against his shins, Isaac's fingers dipped into her hair and threaded across her scalp.

Eleanor closed her eyes and melted into the crashing-wave sound of her hair being folded within itself.

She hadn't felt this pampered since...since Cass. Throughout high school, Cass was her formal-event stylist, whether or not Eleanor asked her to be. Braids, curls, updos, she could do everything—except use the sink to undo her makeup mistakes. One time, she had messed up Eleanor's eyeshadow and, instead of reaching for the washcloth and faucet right next to her, Cass just licked her thumb and wiped off the mistake mom-style.

A chuckle escaped Eleanor.

"Did I mess up?"

"No," she said. "This feels nice."

"How does it look?" He switched the wall panel to mirror mode. She stood up and used her watch's selfie view to see the back of her head.

"Oh, it looks good!"

He laughed. "You sound surprised. I followed a tutorial."

"Well, yeah, but just because you follow directions doesn't mean it always turns out."

He almost looked concerned. "Really?"

"Yeah. Human error, I guess."

* * *

"So how can I best navigate your social anxiety here?" Isaac asked as they approached the front of the line. "Are you more concerned about crowds or loud noises?"

"You're just keeping me company," Eleanor said as they received their event wristbands.

"Which means what, exactly?"

"That's not part of your programming?"

"It is, but it's always tied to something. Playing music to help someone remember. Helping them navigate a busy store. Calming them when they're agitated. I want to make sure I'm doing what you're asking of me."

"Okay." She wrapped her hand around his elbow. "We're going to walk around and listen to street performers and I'm going to eat delicious food. During all that, we'll talk."

Isaac nodded. "I can do that."

"Ooh! Fried ice cream!" Eleanor tapped the food truck's menu monitor then bumped her watch against it to pay. A metal dish with one perfectly golden scoop slid out. She grabbed a metal spoon out of the dispenser.

Isaac eyed it.

"Oh. Is it rude to eat in front of you?" She kicked herself for not asking that a couple weeks ago.

"No, it's just that the sugar content is—"

"Thanks, I don't need to know. You still on Dad's nutrition settings?"

"Yes. We can adjust those too."

They walked a few more steps.

"I'm young, I'm allowed to have some sugar," she said between bites.

"Technically, added sugar is not good for you at any age."

"Well, *technically*"—her voice slipped into the low register she reserved for teasing—"I don't have to listen to you." She finished the treat and slid the bowl and spoon into a washing station.

Isaac broke into an impish grin, like a child who just learned the 7-8-9 joke. "You'd be less cranky if you ate less sugar."

She swung her leg up and kicked him playfully.

Javi

Javi and John started alternating who cooked on Saturdays. (Javi's dishes were always better.) Javi accepted a permanent position at the clinic. The girls' adoption was made official, and they all celebrated. Eventually John felt comfortable enough leaving the girls home with a sitter again, so he and Javi started going to movies, plays, anything that caught their eye. The girls grew and started participating in after-school and summer activities. When Javi traveled to conferences, John watched the dogs; when Javi's clothes needed repairing, John mended them. But Saturdays always stayed the same.

One night Javi woke up on John's couch. When he had fallen asleep, he had both girls nestled in his arms and a movie playing that the girls had already seen nineteen times. Now the TV was off and the girls were gone. John was reading in his armchair.

"Hey," John said softly.

"Girls?" Javi asked sleepily.

"I carried them to bed."

Javi stretched his arms toward John. "You gonna carry me to bed too?"

John laughed. "Not unless you want to throw my back out."

"Mmm, not like that, I don't."

John usually responded to comments like that with an eyeroll and a grin. But this time the remark was met with an awkward, breathless chuckle.

"You know…" John rubbed the back of his neck. "If you're too tired to drive home, you can stay here."

"That's all right, that's what the autopilot is for."

"Right. Sure."

Javi sleepily gathered the dogs, said good night to John, and drove home. As his car pulled onto the two-lane highway, his brain finally clicked John's words into place and he woke up like he had been hit with a shot of espresso.

"Wait, did he just—" He turned to the dogs, but they didn't have an answer.

Eleanor

The sky darkened and thunder threatened. Eleanor and Isaac, returning from a movie, had just made it to her front yard when the downpour began, thick, unrelenting pellets of water instantly soaking Eleanor's skin.

She sprinted as best as she could in her strappy sandals. She reached the front door and fumbled for her keys. When she unlocked the door and pushed it open, she realized Isaac wasn't behind her. She turned and saw his body face-down in the grass. A jolt ran through her.

She ran to him and knelt down, slipping on the wet grass. "Isaac!"

His eyes were closed. He normally must have some sort of glow under his skin, because that was gone. She felt for a pulse and then remembered there wouldn't be one.

She slipped her arms under his armpits and tried to lift him up.

"Dammit-Cass-why-would-you-order-him-so-heavy?"

Her butt hit the soaked grass twice before she found her footing. Slowly, excruciatingly, she got him up the front steps and into the house.

The rain must've shut him off, like in the stories Dad and Papi used to tell of cell phones that weren't waterproof, when they would put them in some—

She dragged Isaac into the kitchen and laid him on the floor. She rifled through the cupboards. She only had one jar of rice.

Wouldn't she have to completely submerge him? Isn't that what Dad and Papi said they did?

Eleanor pulled up her wall panel. Nothing on the customer service page about a soaked robot.

"Hi, I'm Luis," the chat window said. "How can I help you today?"

Eleanor hit the call button. "Hey, Luis. My care-bot got wet. We got hit with a sudden rainstorm and he just shut down."

"Okay. Can I get your name, please, so I can look up your model?"

"Eleanor. Look, I'm not in your system."

The tapping of keys stopped. "Then how do you have—"

"My sister bought my dad one, and now I have him. She bought him five years ago, if that helps."

"A little. That eliminates any models we've released since that time."

"And he might be a refurbished bot, I'm not sure. Look, I just need to know what to do when he shuts down like this. I was going to submerge him in rice, but I only have the one jar. Do I need to buy more?"

"Rice?"

"Yeah, like when cell phones would get wet and people used to..." Her voice trailed off once she realized how stupid it sounded.

"Yeah, don't put rice on him." Luis clacked away. "Looks like you'll need to completely dry him off then get him back into his charger. Towels first, then a hairdryer on the 'low heat' setting. Anything else I can help you with today?"

"Yeah. Why on earth wouldn't you make him waterproof? They're supposed to be able to bathe people, and you'd have to take rain into consideration."

"Right, his hands and forearms are waterproof but, like you said, yours is an older model. We've addressed that concern since."

"Oh. That makes sense."

"If you'd like to get a newer model—"

"Nope."

Eleanor closed the browser. A shiver ripped through her body. She peeled off her wet clothes, toweled off, and changed into lounge pants and a sweatshirt.

Then she grabbed the rest of her towels and got to work.

She lifted Isaac's arms and legs and wrapped towels around them. She draped another over his torso. She lifted his neck and placed a folded towel behind his head. She took a hand towel to his ears, his chin, his eyelids.

Her heart rate finally slowed down. He looked like he was sleeping, the furrowed brow, the almost-pout on his lips. She brushed the hair off his forehead, smoothed an eyebrow with her thumb. Then remembered what she was supposed to be doing.

It seemed like hours until he was dry enough for his charger. She hoisted him up again and dragged him toward his room. She muttered "sorry" every time she bumped him into a doorframe.

There was no way she'd be able to prop him up and back into his charger.

She set him down in the hallway—"Sorry"—and laid his charger on the bedroom floor. She grabbed him under the armpits again and waddled backward toward the charger. She nudged his legs apart to get them on either side of the base. She set his head down so it would click into place, then lifted his legs and arms and clicked them into place.

CHARGING, the top piece read.

She sighed in relief. She pulled herself onto the guest bed and fell asleep face-down.

* * *

The next day, Eleanor was eating lunch by the time Isaac emerged from his room. His eyes were closed, like he was experiencing the worst hangover of his life.

"How are you feeling?" she said quietly.

"BRRRRREAKFAST." It wasn't his voice. It was some horrible, harsh, metallic thing.

Eleanor leapt up. "Okay, you're still recovering." She slipped his arm over her shoulder and tried to lead him back to his room, but his legs didn't move.

"BRRR—"

"I ate breakfast. I just need you to recover."

He still didn't move.

"Go back to charger. *Charger.*"

Finally, his legs began to move. Eleanor guided him back to his room, set his charger upright, and helped him back into it. The light drained from his face once again.

Eleanor's feet were frozen to the carpet. Her chest felt carved out.

"Please get better."

Her watch buzzed. Isaac's eyes wrenched open.

"No, go to sleep. Hey, Cass." Eleanor stepped out of the room and closed the door behind her.

"Why are you whispering?"

"Oh. Um. Isaac's having some issues, so I'm trying to let him recharge without him responding to my voice."

"What's wrong with him?"

"He shut down last night—"

"You *broke* him?"

"I didn't—I don't think so. He got wet so I had to dry him off and he's still recovering."

"What do you mean he got wet? What the hell were you doing?"

"It was raining," Eleanor hissed. "Apparently his model can't take in that much water at once."

"Okay, this is why I wanted to sell him. So you wouldn't break him first."

"Oh, really. You knew when you bought him that I'd take him home and subject him to a downpour?"

"No, but I should've figured you'd find some way to screw this up."

"Yes, because my only goal in life is to make things harder for you. Is that why you called? Your 'Eleanor screwed up' alarm was going off?"

The silence on Cass's end was deafening.

"It's Papi's birthday. I always call on his birthday."

"Shit." Eleanor closed her eyes and hung her head.

"You forgot."

"No, I know what day his birthday is. I just forgot what *today* is. Sorry, the whole Isaac thing really threw me off. Did you celebrate already?"

Dad had always cooked knoephla soup for Papi's birthday. After Papi died, Dad and the girls continued the tradition. Now, Eleanor supposed, they would start celebrating Dad's birthday with Papi's hilachas. Eleanor had decided this year to take Isaac out to eat, so she hadn't asked him to buy any of the ingredients.

"Yeah. Abir and I tried an Indian spin on it this year."

They chatted civilly enough until Cass said she had to go.

Eleanor checked on Isaac. No progress.

She typed a note for him on the wall panel and went to the store. She spent the rest of the day in the kitchen, checking in on Isaac after every imagined noise. She ate by herself, packaged up the leftovers, and did dishes in silence. No music, not today.

She watched Papi's favorite movie but with subtitles instead of volume. She checked on Isaac one more time then went to bed.

* * *

She was so tired the next morning that her brain didn't register the sounds coming from the kitchen. Then she saw Isaac making tea.

"Oh, thank God." She wrapped her arms around him and buried her face in his chest. She soaked in his humming warmth.

Isaac laughed. "What's wrong?"

"You were—I thought I broke you." She realized she was still holding him. She let go.

"The downpour. Yes, I appear to be fully functioning again."

"That's good. Yeah, that's—" She took the mug he handed her. "I'll get you an umbrella, and you can strap it to your belt or something."

"I'll add it to your list." He turned back to making breakfast.

She watched him. Then nodded and sat down in the dining room.

Javi

Nothing seemed to change between them, so Javi put the moment out of his head. Months later, though, he and the dogs were leaving John's house when he heard the front door wrench open behind him.

"I love you," John blurted into the night air.

Javi stared at him, the dogs tugging at their leashes. A moth fluttered across the porch light. John tried to slink back into the house.

"Oh, no, you don't." Javi glanced around him. "Let me get the dogs in the car and the A/C going and then we'll talk."

He walked to the car. He felt his chest inflating; he couldn't stop smiling. He came back to find John sitting sheepishly on the front steps. Javi joined him.

"So what changed?" Javi asked.

John sighed, staring at his hands. "Do you remember that night you fell asleep on the couch? I don't know, something about seeing you like that with the girls, I—it was like sinking into a warm bath. But I didn't know if you still felt the same way—it's been four years since we met—so I kept it to myself. It was just easier, right? We already had a good thing going, so why would I mess that up? But..." John took a breath. "Things only stay the same if nothing changes."

Javi gave him a look.

John rolled his eyes. "I mean, you could get a different job and move. Or you could meet someone else. And it just...hit me how badly I don't want to lose you."

"I wouldn't worry too much about someone else coming along."

"Oh, please, you got an ass like a pair of cantaloupes."

Javi laughed so hard he probably woke the girls upstairs.

"Not that someone would only be interested in your body," John added hurriedly. "Obviously, they'd love your heart and your mind and your sense of humor—"

Javi straddled him, tilted his head back, and kissed him. John melted into the kiss.

When they broke for air, John's eyes stayed closed and his breath shuddered. "Bedroom, or..." His voice trailed off.

Javi grinned. "There's no rush." He kissed him again then stood up. "Plus, I have a feeling you love watching me walk away."

"I'm never going to live that down, am I?"

"Nope!" Javi did an exaggerated strut back to his car, grateful that John couldn't see the stupid giddy grin on his face. He could only imagine what John's looked like right now.

Eleanor

Normally Eleanor avoided bars. They combined three of her least favorite things: crowds, drunk people, and crowds of drunk people. But one in town was hosting a Nineties Night, and she had found a windbreaker in Isaac's size and a sunflower-print dress with spaghetti straps and a white T-shirt for herself.

"Isaac, guess what we're doing on Saturday?"

She told him about the event and showed him the jacket.

"Sounds good, I can save you a table."

"No, you're dancing with me. If I wanted to dance by myself, I'd go by myself."

"Oh." He almost looked nervous. "That is not one of my skills."

"Mine neither, but that doesn't stop me." He still eyed the jacket apprehensively, so she added, "Hey, we have six days. That's plenty of time to practice."

* * *

The night of, she took Isaac's hand and led him into the bar, but then she stopped. Oh, it was crowded. She forgot this is what other people did on Saturday. She tried to nope right out of there, but she bumped into him.

She couldn't hear what he said over the music, but he gave her a smile, so she turned around and beelined for the dance floor. They had practiced all week, but Isaac seemed to feel more comfortable copying her moves. She loved how seriously he seemed to be taking this. Thankfully, "Mambo No. 5" came on, so they could practice the swing moves they'd learned.

"Okay, I gotta sit down," she said when the song ended. She could barely hear herself, so she signed to him. She had been relearning ASL.

"Do you want something to drink?" he signed back.

She gave him her order and left the dance floor. She found an empty table and sat down. Her heart was thumping, she couldn't catch her breath, but she was smiling. Her stomach was feather-light. She couldn't remember the last time she danced like this. Felt like this.

She spotted Isaac and waved him over. Her stomach flipped at his grin. He placed the strawberry daquiri in front of her and set the glass of water in front of himself—for appearances, she'd told him on the way there, and so she could stay hydrated.

A woman in a slip dress approached them. The music had quieted down slightly, transitioning into the next song.

"Hey, can I join you?" she asked Isaac.

Isaac looked to Eleanor for an answer, but the woman sat down before Eleanor's brain could register what was happening.

"I'm Lexa."

"I'm Isaac and this is Eleanor."

Eleanor gave a wave that was less of a hello and more of a "What are you doing..."

"Oh, that's so nice of you to take your kid sister out!"

The blood roared in Eleanor's ears, so loudly she couldn't hear anything else Lexa was saying to Isaac. She wanted to say, "We're together," but it would just sound petulant and forced, especially since she'd have to shout to be heard over the louder-again music.

Lexa wasn't even looking at her. Her shoulder was facing Eleanor and the rest of her faced Isaac.

What was Eleanor supposed to do? Tap him on the shoulder? Drag him back onto the dance floor?

If they played a slow song, Eleanor would grab his hand. Did bars play slow songs? Considering she couldn't hear either of the people at her table, she guessed not.

Eleanor chugged her drink while Lexa chatted Isaac up.

And what was Isaac doing? He told what's-her-face they weren't siblings, right? That they came here together and they lived together.

Was she—was she *flirting* with him? You could do that? You could walk up to a guy who was obviously sitting with somebody else and just...flirt with him and touch his arm and—

She was touching his arm. Just wrapping her fingers around his wrist like she owned him. Couldn't she feel the metal frame through his sweater and jacket?

And Isaac was just sitting there with that stupid placid look on his face.

Eleanor's sternum was burning. Her glass was empty, and that was a problem. She pulled up the order-machine in the middle of the table, tapped her watch against it to open a tab, and ordered shots.

HOW MANY? the screen asked.

How many indeed. How many until this night disappeared.

A server brought three over and set them in the middle of the table.

"Oh, you ordered shots for us?" Lexa shouted over the music.

"Nope." Eleanor slid the three glasses toward herself.

"Eleanor, the alcohol content—"

She took a shot.

"Oh, that's so sweet of you to worry, she's fine."

She took another shot.

Lexa kept talking to him, song after song after song after song. Eleanor caught a snippet of their conversation between a Gin Blossoms song fading out and a 702 song fading in.

"I'll have to get your number."

"I have a private number only shared with designated contacts."

"Then what's your watch for?" Lexa teased.

"It's just decorative." He tapped the screen, which didn't light up.

"Oh, low-tech, I like it. Come on, let's dance."

"Oh—"

"C'mon, just one song..." Lexa pulled Isaac from the table.

Who did Lexa think she was, just walking up to a table where two people were already talking, already having fun without her? Who did that? Eleanor and Isaac were obviously together. They walked in together, they danced together, he brought her drinks, they were sitting together. Anyone should be able to see that.

And yet Eleanor was sitting alone while Lexa and Isaac were somewhere on the dance floor. She didn't know what would've been worse: having to watch them dance, watching Lexa swish her perfect hair around, swing her hips, pull him close, while Isaac just smiled clueless—or the reality that Lexa had pulled him somewhere into the thicket of dancers where Eleanor couldn't see them.

Nope, not seeing them was definitely worse. Lexa could pull him into a dark corner or a bathroom or take him home, and he'd let her. Would he? He might, especially if she worded it just vaguely enough that he thought he was helping her with something. And he'd probably look up the health benefits of kissing or…other things.

Eleanor snorted at the idea of Lexa trying to undress him and realizing that the clothes were sewn into the rubbery skin, that there was nothing underneath anyway—

It stopped being funny.

Eleanor had to find him. She didn't care what kind of scene she made—it was a bar and she had been drinking; it was practically required of her.

Her fingers needed two attempts to hit the Close Tab button on the order-machine, and her wrist struggled to tap her watch against the screen to pay. She threw back the last shot and stood up on the rungs of her chair. She wobbled.

Then she saw him returning, Lexa right at his heels. Eleanor sat back down.

"That's it?" Lexa said when they sat down. Her tone was playful but her smile was strained.

"You said one song."

Eleanor guessed that he was taking in the sight of the empty shot glasses with concern, but she was glaring at Lexa.

"So what are you doing after this?" Lexa asked, recomposing herself.

"I'm taking Eleanor home." His tone was as pleasant as ever.

"And after that?"

Eleanor slapped her hands on the table. "We're leaving." She pushed herself upward and immediately toppled over.

Isaac caught her and set her on her feet. Without another glance or word at Lexa, he walked Eleanor toward the door, his arm tight around her waist.

They walked to the bus stop in silence, Eleanor fuming, Isaac blithely ignorant. When the bus arrived, Eleanor threw herself onto an aisle-facing seat. Isaac sat down next to her. She slid two seats away from him. She leaned against the pole and stewed in her anger; it roiled her stomach and burned her cheeks.

"Are you upset?" Isaac asked.

She whipped around to glare at him. But her stomach lurched just as she opened her mouth, and jewel-red vomit spewed onto the floor.

The other people on the bus scattered away from the mess like marbles from a dropped bag.

Isaac didn't jump or flinch. He just pulled a ponytail holder off his wrist and secured the strands of Eleanor's hair that hadn't been twisted into butterfly clips.

The bus's wet-vac disks spun out of their ports and cleaned up the mess.

Isaac rubbed her back until they reached their stop. Without a word she leaned on his arm as they walked. He led her into the house and straight into the bathroom.

"Do you feel like you're going to throw up again?"

She shook her head. Thought about it. Shrugged. She avoided his eyes.

"Can I help clean you up?"

"I can do it myself." She tried to pull off her dress but hit her elbow on the bathroom door and almost tipped over. He steadied her.

"Fine," she grumbled.

He peeled the dress, T-shirt, and sandals off her and placed them in the shower-tub. He sat her down on the tub's six-inch-wide ledge so that she faced the sink, only a couple feet away in her small bathroom. She tried to focus on the feeling of the bathmat beneath the soles of her feet. He wet a rag in the sink and cleaned the vomit off her chin and feet. Eleanor leaned her left shoulder against one of the shower-tub's walls, miserable.

"That was supposed to be us."

Isaac glanced at her. "What do you mean?"

"We were supposed to dance and talk but she just showed up and ruined everything. You and I were supposed to have a nice night together and then come home and cuddle on the couch and she ruined it."

The wet rag on her feet stopped moving. Isaac gave her a long, unreadable look, then he dropped the rag into the tub.

"I'll get you some pajamas." He left.

Acid burned in the back of her throat. Eleanor wiped the corners of her eyes.

He returned with pajama shorts and one of Papi's concert tees. He threaded her arms through the sleeves and pulled the shirt over her head. As he placed her feet into the shorts, her head tipped forward and tapped against his.

"Put your arms around my neck," Isaac said.

She did, and he effortlessly lifted her just high enough to pull the shorts up. Then he took the butterfly clips and ponytail holder out of her hair.

"Are you ready for bed?"

She nodded. Then she remembered. "Teeth."

He got her toothbrush ready and stood in the doorframe—she insisted on brushing her own teeth. Then he helped her stand up so she could rinse out the toothpaste and the aftertaste of puke. He took her hands and guided her out of the bathroom and into her room. Isaac pulled back the sheets for her and helped her into bed. He filled her old backpack with books from the shelf under her nightstand and strapped it onto her.

"I don't wanna go to school..."

"This is to make sure you stay on your side, so you don't roll onto your back and choke on your vomit."

"I'm not that drunk."

"I'm not risking it." He helped her into the recovery position.

"Oh, dress," she said after he tucked her in. The words slid milkshake-slow across her tongue.

"I'll wash your clothes and rinse off your shoes tonight."

"Thank you," she slurred into the pillow.

He brushed the hair off her forehead. She closed her eyes at the touch. "Thanks for letting me take care of you."

"S'okay."

She fell asleep instantly.

* * *

Isaac was bound to ask about last night. That was why Eleanor was lying in bed long after she had woken up. That and the throbbing headache.

Would he just blame the anger on the alcohol? Or file it away under weird human things like repeatedly singing one lyric after hearing a song on the radio? Or would he know she had been jealous? Still was jealous. Just the thought of Lexa's hand on his arm made her stomach churn. Well, that and the rum and tequila.

She sighed and got up. Slowly.

In the living and dining rooms, all the lights were off and the curtains were closed, but so much sunlight seeped in through the thin curtains that she could've been standing on a theater stage. Eleanor grimaced against the brightness.

"Good morning," Isaac said, his volume at its lowest setting.

"Morning." Her voice was a thick rug on her tongue. She sat on the floor. She tried lying down—nope, that was worse. She sat up again and leaned against the side of the couch until the dizziness went away.

"I didn't make you breakfast yet. The suggestions I found online sounded unhealthy." He handed her a glass of water and some ibuprofen. He knelt next to her as she drank. He didn't mention Lexa or Eleanor's behavior last night. She didn't bring either of them up.

"Thanks for taking care of me last night," she said, her voice raspy.

His smile almost started the dizziness again. "That wasn't so bad, was it?"

Her lips twitched into a smile. "Don't get used to it," she muttered into her glass.

Javi

Javi walked downstairs. The girls were old enough now that John had moved himself from the guest bedroom upstairs into the main bedroom on the first floor.

"They're asleep," Javi said quietly to John.

"Asleep-asleep?"

Javi nodded.

They closed the space between them immediately, kissing each other's mouths and necks, running their fingers through the other's hair, drinking each other in.

"I've been thinking about this all day," Javi breathed, as he walked John to the bedroom door.

John stepped on a dog toy, which let out a long, dying squeak.

"No," Javi said. "No, no, no, no, no…"

The dogs, who had all been asleep in the kitchen, skittered into the living room.

"You get them settled. I have to use the bathroom anyway," John said. He disappeared into the bedroom.

Javi knelt down and faced the dogs. "Don't you dare screw this up for me," he hissed.

Javi slipped inside the room, undressed, and climbed into bed. Singing "Waiting for Tonight" under his breath, he practiced the best way to dramatically fling the covers off himself.

But the bathroom door stayed closed.

Javi got out of bed and knocked on the door. "John?"

"Just a minute." His voice cracked.

"If you don't want to—"

"No, I want to, I'm just—" He opened the door and saw Javi's body. "Oh, come on."

John closed the door. When he opened it again, Javi greeted him with a ridiculous, sexy lean against the doorframe that made him snort.

"You were saying?" Javi said.

John looked away and rubbed the back of his neck. "I'm nervous. I didn't think I would be, but I haven't done this since college and I just got into my head."

"John, what do you want to do instead?"

"I want to do this—"

"If you have to talk yourself into it, we're not doing it," Javi said gently. "What do you want to do instead?"

John thought for a moment. "Can I just hold you until we fall asleep together?"

"Of course." Javi pulled him in for a kiss, and John sank into it.

The next morning, Javi rolled over and found the girls staring at him from the edge of the bed. He startled.

"Will you make us breakfast?" Eleanor said in that kid whisper that was still really loud.

He glanced down and sighed with relief that a bedsheet was covering his lower half. "Sure, just let me get—"

Cassie thumped a shirt and pants onto the bed.

"—dressed."

He sent them out of the room and pulled on his clothes. When he stepped out of the bedroom, he found the girls already sitting on the kitchen stools. He poured them some cereal and made himself some coffee.

"Do you live here now?" Eleanor asked. "Are you and Dad getting married?"

"They're already married, dummy."

"No, they're not," Eleanor protested, her voice rising. "They don't have rings."

"I don't know, hon—"

"Can I be flower girl?" Cassie chirped.

Eleanor slammed her hand on the counter. "I want to be flower girl!"

"You can both be flower girls," Javi hissed, flattening himself against the counter. "Just don't wake your father."

"What do we call you now?" Eleanor asked.

"'Javi' is fine."

"How do you say 'Dad' in Spanish?" Cassie asked.

"Papá."

"Papa?"

"No, that's 'potato.' How about Papi?"

Cassie, who had just watched *The Wizard of Oz* that week, responded with "Popppiesss…"

Javi smiled; he would explain later that the first letter sounded more like a B than a P. John finally emerged from the bedroom. Javi's stomach flipped at the sight of him.

Cassie waved him over. "You and Poppy are getting married and we're gonna be flower girls!"

John looked at Javi for clarification. Javi just waved him off and turned to his coffee. "That's what you get for sleeping in so late," he muttered. But his thoughts were on the gold rings already sitting in his online shopping cart.

Eleanor

Isaac rapped his knuckles against the wall above the couch. "Can I interrupt for a moment?"

"Yeah, one second." She slipped in a bookmark and closed her book. "What's up?"

"I was thinking about last Saturday and was wondering if you wanted to do those kinds of events more frequently."

Eleanor raised an eyebrow. "More events where I throw up on the bus?"

"No, events like dinner and movies. I recognize we already do those things, but do you want to pick a night every week where we go out?"

Her stomach flipped at the last two words. "Oh, sure. Um, not Friday, because I never want to do anything after work. Saturday?"

"Saturday works for me. Do you want to plan the event, or do you want me to?"

"Uh...I'll let you know if I have ideas. Otherwise, you can plan it if you want. Just run it by me first. Like I'm not going skydiving or anything."

"Oh, I'm not compatible with skydiving. Great! I'll start planning." He disappeared back into the kitchen.

Eleanor stared after him, bemused.

Javi

Javi moved out of his apartment into John's house. He picked up the rhythm of getting the girls ready for school, helping with homework, splitting the chores. One day, Javi arrived home from work late, disgruntled, and wet.

"What happened to your coat?" John asked. Javi could barely hear him over the girls and the dogs greeting him.

"Some idiot in the parking lot thought speeding through a mud puddle would be a good idea," Javi muttered.

He peeled off the ankle-length jacket and handed it to John. John headed to the laundry room while Javi said a quick hello to the girls, who were leaning over the back of the couch and each telling him a different story at the same time. He suddenly remembered and patted his pants pockets.

It wasn't there.

He bolted across the kitchen to the laundry room; the dogs chased after him, barking. "Hey, I need to empty my pockets fir—"

But John had beaten him to it. He was holding the box. "Is this—"

"No." Javi snatched it out of John's hand and shoved it into his pants pocket. He had been carrying it on him ever since he had ordered it and had it delivered to his office. The plan had worked until now.

"Were you going to—" John sounded breathless.

"Not yet. You didn't see anything."

John broke into a wide, thrilled smile. The dogs had finally stopped barking. "Of course I'll marry you."

"No!" Javi hissed, pointing a threatening finger at John. "This is not the proposal!"

"Who's getting married?" Cassie yelled.

Two sets of feet thundered toward the laundry room. The dogs started barking again.

"No one," Javi said over the noise. "Not yet."

"Why not?" Eleanor asked.

"Because I haven't proposed yet."

"What are you waiting for?" Cassie asked. She was still yelling even after the dogs had calmed down.

"The right moment."

The girls waited expectantly.

"No, girls, proposals should be special. They need to be planned. They need to be a good story to tell loved ones. They need choreography of 'I Will Be There' by Britney Spears."

"C'mon, please?" Eleanor said.

"Do it, do it," Cassie started chanting.

John was laughing.

Javi growled. "Fine." He knelt but turned toward the girls. He took their hands. "Cassie and Eleanor, would you do me the honor of becoming my daughters and being the flower girls at our wedding?"

They screamed their approval, wrenched Javi into a hug, and ran upstairs, Javi assumed to try on every dress they owned. The dogs stampeded after them. For some reason, Cassie was yelling, "We're going to Disney World!"

Javi sank to the floor, his elbows on his knees and the heels of his palms digging into his eyes. He felt John sit next to him, their shoulders touching.

"This is not the proposal," Javi said into his arms.

"For what it's worth, this is a good story."

Javi ignored him. "And now I have to scrap everything I planned and start over. It's not going to mean anything if you know the song and what the wedding rings look like."

"I didn't look inside."

"Thank you," Javi said quietly.

"If you want me to take the pressure off, I can—"

"If you take this away from me, I will slash your tires."

"Yes'm."

Eleanor

Something changed, but Eleanor had a hard time naming it. For example, before, when she and Isaac were listening to music in the kitchen, she danced and he blithely obliged her occasional hip checks. Now, when she started dancing, he stopped whatever he was doing, reached for her hands, and twirled her around.

Eleanor had spent the week on the verge of calling her sister and asking her, but she didn't know how to describe it. And some part of her was convinced that putting it into words would pop the bubble.

But, as usual, life decided for her.

"Hey, quick question," Cass said when Eleanor answered the call. "Do we still have Dad and Papi's Halloween photos? I thought I'd turn them into a collage."

"Yeah, I'll look."

She went into the basement and started digging through storage totes. The sisters small-talked about work, and Eleanor remembered to ask how Abir was doing.

"And how's Isaac?" Cass asked. "Fully recovered?"

"Yep, back to normal. Well, he's...Yeah. He's good."

"What?"

"No, nothing's wrong. He's just—I don't know how to describe it."

"What?"

Eleanor sighed and repositioned herself so she could keep an eye on the stairs, in case Isaac came back in from yardwork. "It's almost like he went from caregiver mode to...I don't know, boyfriend mode."

She shouldn't have said it. Cass's voice switched to a cackle.

"Oh-ho-ho!"

"Not like that!" Eleanor hissed. "Like he bought me flowers—"

"With your money."

"With my money. And dances with me in the kitchen and asked if I wanted a shoulder massage the other night. And not that those can't be friend things, but it just feels different."

"What do you think changed? Or when?"

"I don't know, sometime after Nineties Night." She sat down. "Oh, no."

"What?"

"I got drunk and made an absolute idiot of myself. I must've said something stupid to him when he was cleaning vomit off me."

"Hmm."

"What do I do?"

"I'm not answering that for you. What do you *want* to do?"

"I don't know..."

"Well, how do you feel about him?"

"How the hell would I know?" She heard a door open upstairs. "Gotta go. I'll find the pictures and put them in the mail for you."

"For what it's worth, you have my blessing to switch into girlfriend mode. If you want that."

Eleanor rolled her eyes. "I'm hanging up now."

"Love you too. Beep bop boop."

How did she feel about him? Honestly, it was like hot water on freezing skin.

* * *

"Hey, don't make supper tonight," Eleanor told Isaac. "There's a new restaurant with outdoor seating and I want to check it out."

She slipped into her red dress. Her chest felt light, buzzing. Is this what other people felt like all the time? That they were stepping into a night of possibility? It was just dinner, but to Eleanor it felt like a kid's Christmas morning. Maybe they'd go dancing afterward. She savored the thought until she remembered that night at the bar. No, somewhere quiet this time. A single streetlight in a corner of a park. Soft music spilling out of someone's apartment. She'd look into his eyes and trip over her own feet.

Isaac knocked on the door, bringing her back to reality. "You ready?"

They took the bus and walked from the bus stop to the restaurant. Eleanor took a deep breath. "Can we hold hands?" she asked him.

He smiled and held out his hand, and she laced her fingers through his. He squeezed her thumb with his thumb and forefinger.

"You're testing my oxygen levels, aren't you?"

"I don't think your hands are supposed to be this cold," he said.

She laughed.

They ate dinner in the outdoor section. Isaac must've looked up how to flirt, because he kept complimenting her and she just blushed and shook her head and grinned.

She spotted a woman across the street walking a pit bull.

"Oh, look at that dog!" Eleanor cupped her face in her hands.

"You grew up with dogs, didn't you?"

"Yeah. Four total, but not all at once. Dad liked them, but they were Papi's dogs. We never got another one after the last one passed away."

"Why don't you have one? You seem fond of them."

"Oh, I love them, I just—I don't know, I guess I just fell out of the habit of having one around."

Isaac didn't respond. He was watching something over Eleanor's shoulder. She'd never seen that kind of intensity in his eyes before. It scared her for some reason. She followed his gaze and saw a family. The teenager—either high school- or college-age—had cerebral palsy, and the spacing between tables was too narrow for his wheelchair to pass through.

Isaac got up. "I'm going to help them."

"Ask first..." Her voice drifted away.

He spoke to the teenager, who nodded. Isaac began moving aside empty tables and chairs and got the family situated. His whole body seemed to buzz. Eleanor shivered.

"Is there anything else I can help you with?" she heard him say.

"Are you the owner?" the mother asked.

"No, I just wanted to help. If that's not rude," he added.

ANY DESSERT TONIGHT? the order-machine on the table chirped.

Eleanor tapped no and paid the bill.

Isaac returned to the table. His eyes were bright; even his cheeks seemed flushed, like he'd sprinted over here. It took him a moment to remember Eleanor. "What now?" he asked.

"Let's just go home," she said quietly.

* * *

The next morning, Eleanor could smell something burning before she entered the kitchen. A slight haze hung around the light fixture.

Eleanor moved the skillet of black pancakes, turned off the burner, and cracked open the windows. Isaac hadn't moved from his spot in front of the stovetop. His face was blank, his eyes unfocused but intense.

At least she had caught it before the smoke alarm—The smoke alarm started blaring.

Isaac startled.

Eleanor grabbed a chair and started fanning smoke away from the alarm until it calmed down.

Isaac's eyes locked onto Eleanor and his smile was too wide. "Good morning! I thought I'd make pancakes." He took in the sight of the stovetop. "Oh. I must've burned them. I'm sorry."

"Are you all right?"

"Yes! Yes." His smile grew wider but his eyes were harried. "I was focused on something else. I'm sorry, breakfast will be late."

He reached for the bowl of batter, but Eleanor took it. "No, I'll get it."

"No, it's my job—"

"Let me do this," she said quietly, gently. "I can make pancakes, let me do this."

He let go and nodded, still distracted. "Okay, I'll—find something else to do. I'll clean the guest room."

"Isaac, are you sure you're okay?"

"Yes. Fine." He gave her a close-lipped smile and left.

Javi

Six years had passed. The wedding, the honeymoon, the family-moon that came first because Cassie (who now went by Cass) had insisted on a trip to Disney World. Birthdays, Christmases, hockey games, school plays. Lazy summers, long winters, hectic mornings, quiet evenings. All blended together: the beautiful, the frustrating, the calm, the chaotic.

It had been an ordinary day until the drive home from work. John and the girls were already home with the dogs. Javi was running late.

He noticed something was wrong before the car did. The turn onto the gravel road was coming up but the car was going the same speed.

A chill coursed through Javi's body.

The brakes had failed. The car wouldn't slow down in time to make the turn safely. He was about to spin onto a gravel road at 70 miles an hour.

A beep from the dashboard signaled the malfunction.

Javi flailed at the settings, trying to set a new destination so the car could keep driving straight. But it was too late.

Prayers he hadn't muttered since middle school flooded his head.

Dios te salve, María, llena eres de gracia, el Señor es contigo. Bendita tú eres entre todas las mujeres, y bendito es el fruto de tu vientre, Jesús.

He'd never see John or the girls again. His dogs would never know where he had gone.

Santa María, Madre de Dios, ruega por nosotros pecadores, ahora y en la hora de nuestra muerte—

Eleanor

"Isaac?" Eleanor called out when she came home from work.

The house was spotless. Everything had been tucked away. Curtains were straightened. Even the walls looked like they had been scrubbed. The whole place smelled like a hospital. Eleanor searched his and her rooms and circled through the living room and kitchen.

Something thudded in the basement.

"Isaac?"

She rushed downstairs. A storage tote must've fallen off the metal shelving, because one was broken open on the floor. Isaac must've fallen too, because he was sitting up.

"I apologize for the noise," he said, scooping Dad's books off the floor. "I was reorganizing and this one fell." He clicked the lid back onto the cracked storage tote. He looked at Eleanor, now at his side, as if fully processing her. "I haven't started your dinner yet. I got started on this project and wanted to finish first. I'm so sorry."

"You don't need to apologize." The skin above Isaac's eye was cut. Eleanor could see a sliver of metal frame underneath. "You're torn." She knelt and reached for his face, but he ignored her. "I'll look up how to fix it, maybe there's a glue we can buy..."

"I'm not doing enough."

"What?"

"I'm not doing enough. There's so much I should be doing—"

"No, you're doing fine," Eleanor said. "You know you don't need to do anything for me."

He froze, his eyes shining. Eleanor leaned back. "You're right. You don't need me. I just have to find someone who needs help with activities of daily living."

"What?" The word barely left her mouth.

He stood up and walked away. "Another dementia patient or someone with a disability. Someone who needs 24-hour care..." His footsteps on the stairs drowned out his muttering.

Eleanor was frozen to the basement floor. Only when pain shot through her knee did she get up.

She found him sitting in front of the wall panel. He was serious. He was looking for someone else. Her chest tightened and her eyes grew hot. She wouldn't let him see her like this. Not that he'd even processed that she had walked into the living room.

She went into the bathroom and closed the door, leaning against it. She could feel her breath quickening and growing jagged. She needed to calm down. She glanced at the sheet of paper Isaac had hung up a while ago, cheerfully listing self-care tips.

She plugged the tub and turned on the faucets. She found a container of Epsom salts but her hands shook so badly that the open bag fell into the water.

"*Shit. Shit.*" She shut off the faucets and fished out the bag. She pulled the plug and reached under the sink for some cleaning rags.

There was a knock on the door. "Eleanor?"

She didn't want him to see her like this, but avoiding him would make it seem like she was doing worse than she was. "Yeah." Her voice cracked.

He opened the door and took in the sight of the tub. He knelt beside her. "I can clean that up—"

"Have to start doing this for myself anyway." The words snaked out of her.

He sat in silence while she cleaned.

"I...spoke out of turn earlier," he said.

Eleanor kept her eyes on the tub.

"My protocols don't allow me to transfer ownership to another family. Only the owner can do that."

She glanced at him; her breath caught in her throat.

"Cassandra is still the owner. I put in a request to her but she has not responded yet. Given the time difference, she is most likely asleep. I can withdraw the request."

Eleanor's heart sped up but her stomach hollowed.

"If you want me to stay, I'll stay."

Of course she wanted him to stay. That was all she wanted when she looked at him. But then she remembered his eyes that night at the café and again in the kitchen while the pancakes burned.

She glanced away. "I'm not making you stay."

The silence in the room ballooned.

"You'll meet new people," he said softly.

"New people," she scoffed. "New people? I can't even hold on to the old ones." Before Isaac could protest, she continued, "No, no one from high school stayed in touch. I don't hang out with anyone outside of work. Dad and Papi died, Cass flew halfway around the world to get away from me." She laughed mirthlessly. "And now I'm being left by a fucking robot!" She threw the cleaning rag against the opposite wall of the tub.

Isaac's body stiffened. He stood up.

"Isaac, I didn't mean..."

The door clicked softly behind him.

She left the bathroom and found him seated at the wall panel again. She leaned against the arm of the couch and studied him for a minute.

"Did you find someone?" she asked quietly.

He turned around and gazed at her for a moment. "Yes, I found a family. We met them that night at the café. The oldest child is starting college this fall but is having trouble finding a full-time caregiver in order to live in the dorm. Again, I can't do anything until I hear from Cassandra, but I explained the situation to her."

She nodded and stared down at her arms folded across her chest. She remembered his forehead.

"Do you have a repair kit or something?"

He turned around. "Yes, in the charger. I'll get it."

He went to his room. She tried not to look at the wall panel. When he returned, she held out her hand. "Can I do it?"

He nodded and handed her the kit. He sat so she could reach him more easily.

She held the skin together and wiped on the glue.

"Do I need to hold it in place until it dries?" she asked.

"Yes, just for a minute."

They waited in silence. Gingerly he placed a hand on her waist. "I am sorry."

"Me too." She could feel the tears threatening to surface. She avoided his eyes.

John

"Has anyone heard from Papi?" John asked the girls.

They shook their heads.

"He should be home by now." John called Javi's phone, but it went to voicemail. Even on the days Javi worked late, he was never this late. "I'll drive to the clinic and check on him. Maybe he's having car trouble. And phone trouble."

There was a knock at the front door. The dogs barked. Had Javi locked himself out? No, he would've come in through the garage door, which they only locked at night or when they all left the house.

"No, no bark," John said. He stepped out onto the porch but kept the dogs inside. Joey was great with people, but JC growled at strangers, thinking he had to protect the girls.

He saw the uniform first, then realized this was a former student—Nia—no, Naya—from quite a few years ago. She recognized him too; then she glanced down at her notes and appeared to double-check something. Her face fell. His stomach did as well, although he didn't know why.

"Hi, Mr. Lane. Is this the Ruiz residence too?"

"What happened?" He had a guess, but he wanted so badly to be wrong.

She fidgeted. "May I come in?"

"Not with the dogs, I'm sorry. What happened?"

Naya took a deep breath and checked her notes—anything to avoid looking at him. "There's been an accident."

John's legs started shaking.

"A car accident. Dr. Javier Ruiz de la Rosa—"

John couldn't get any air into his lungs.

"—It looks like the braking mechanism failed when he was trying to turn." She was crying now. "If it's any consolation, we think it was a quick—" She shook her head. "I'm so sorry. Is there anyone in the house I need to tell?"

"No, I'll tell them," John said, his voice empty.

Naya nodded, a little relieved. John imagined this was the first time she'd had to deliver news like this. Once she stepped off the porch, John gathered the strength to turn the door handle. He stepped inside, making sure to keep the dogs in. They were still barking.

The girls stared at him as he walked back to the kitchen, but he couldn't speak. He stood across from where they were sitting at the counter. The sobs in his chest were threatening to overflow. He was drowning; something was clawing him down. The dogs finally quieted.

"Something hap—" He couldn't.

"Papi's dead, isn't he?" Eleanor's voice was quiet but abrupt. Like she had always worried this shoe would drop.

John nodded.

The silence hung in the air for only a moment, but its presence was thick and choking. This was worse, this was so much worse than hearing the news himself.

Cass's face crumpled. She sprinted around the counter, threw her arms around John, and buried her face into his neck. His own tears started; he couldn't catch his breath. Eleanor stared at a spot on the counter, her face immobile. She pushed back her chair—an ugly, scraping sound—and thundered upstairs.

John heard her bedroom door slam and objects being hurled across the room. Eleanor screamed out in rage.

Eleanor

The next day, Cass shot Eleanor a text explaining Isaac's request and asking if she was okay with it. Eleanor stared at it for a couple minutes. One word, two letters, and nothing would change. But that wasn't true, was it? She and Isaac couldn't go back to what they had before, now that she knew what he wanted.

She texted back: *Yep.*

Do you want to talk about it?

No, Eleanor texted. *It's fine.*

Her stomach churned.

* * *

On the first day of the fall semester, they rented a truck and drove to Cooke's dorm. Isaac seemed to struggle to say something. "Eleanor, when there's a transfer of ownership, care-bots undergo a factory reset."

Eleanor glanced at him, confused.

"So I'll need to delete all the information about you and your family. For privacy reasons."

Her stomach plunged. "You're going to forget us."

"Yes." The silence pressed down on Eleanor's chest. "I'll wait until we've set up the charger if that works for you. Then I'll contact Cassandra so she can order the reset and transfer ownership."

They pulled into a Welcome Weekend loading zone and unloaded the charger onto the sidewalk. Eleanor waited for him on the curb while he closed the rental truck's tailgate. He seemed to hesitate a moment before reaching into his pocket. "I understand goodbyes can be difficult," he said, "but having closure can be helpful. I printed up some strategies that might be useful—"

Eleanor kissed him. She heard a sheet of paper flutter to the ground as he wrapped his arms around her. Part of her wondered if he was looking up how to kiss. She didn't mind; this was a first for her too.

She broke off the kiss and pulled him into a tight hug. She kept her eyes squeezed shut.

"You ready?" he said.

She nodded and loosened her grip. Her throat was closing in on itself.

His hand grazed her cheek as he crossed to the charger. Together they carried it into the building and into Room 106. There they found Isaac's new owner.

Cooke, using the computer on his chair to speak, had them set the charger down in the suite's other room. Isaac stayed back to set it up.

"I'm Eleanor. It's nice to meet you."

Cooke jerked his head toward the window. "Were you the one making out with him just now?"

"I gotta go."

But she bumped into his mother, who was carrying in storage totes.

"Oh, sorry."

"You must be Eleanor. Cassandra said we'd be meeting you. I'm Tarana."

"Nice to meet you." Her voice was getting raspier by the minute.

"I already have your sister's info," Tarana continued. "I'll transfer the money to her now."

Eleanor's stomach twinged.

Isaac came back into the room and spoke to Cooke. "The charger's set up. We can program it to whatever hours you don't need me, so that can be at night or during your classes."

"During classes, but does it have to be one chunk of time?" Cooke said. "Because I'll be fine in class, but I'll need help using the bathroom between classes."

"We can set it up so I recharge during classes but meet up with you in between. You can sync me up to your watch and allow me access to your schedule. And we can change it as your schedule changes each semester. And what's your name?"

"Tarana. I'm Cooke's mother."

Eleanor sidled toward the door.

"And you are?"

She froze. Isaac's eyes looked right through her, that same placid gaze from day one.

"Eleanor." Her voice splintered.

He shook her hand. "Eleanor," he said, like he was tasting the word for the first time. "And how do you know the Walkers?"

"I was just helping them move in—"

"You're crying." He was still holding her hand. "Can I—?"

"No, you know, it's just—first day of college." She let go. "I need to head out, though. It was nice to meet you, Tarana. Cooke, you have my number if you have any...tech questions."

She left without looking at Isaac.

She set the truck to return to the rental company and took the bus home. She wasn't sure why she didn't just take the truck, but something about the bus made more sense in that moment. One leg started shaking so hard it was bouncing; her breath shuddered. The tears came out hot and fast, like a dam had burst. She only had a vague understanding the other passengers could see her.

Once home, she curled up onto the floor and let her crying have the volume she had tried to avoid on the bus.

After a few minutes, she sat up and texted Cass, "Can I call you tomorrow?"

Eleanor got off the floor and, without looking to her left, went into the bathroom to wash her face. Finally, she made herself look in Isaac's room. He had draped the apron over the bed.

She stared at it. Had he not liked it? Did he not think he'd need it, since Cooke would be living off dining hall food? Was he just leaving her something to remember him by?

Like she would forget him anytime soon.

She slipped the apron over her head, entered the kitchen, and made herself something to eat.

* * *

On Monday, Eleanor put in her two weeks' notice at work and applied for a job at the animal shelter, mostly working the front desk but other duties as assigned. One day, about a month after she started the new job, she took a walk along the row of dog kennels. Most of the dogs gave booming barks or excited yips, but one dog was quiet.

This one plastered himself to his dog bed, glancing at Eleanor then away, his tail thumping shyly. A small sign on his kennel told employees, volunteers, and visitors that this dog was skittish around strangers. Another sign, which every kennel featured, gave more information about the dog, such as name, age, and breed. This one had been named Chris.

Eleanor crouched down next to the kennel and smiled softly. The dog's tail thumped hopefully.

"Hey, Chris," she murmured.

She could feel her heart start to heal.

ACKNOWLEDGEMENTS

Thank you to William Tracy and the Space Wizard Science Fantasy team. You were so easy to work with and so helpful with your edits and questions. Thanks for taking a chance on *Isaac*. Thanks to MoorBooks for the awesome cover.

Thanks to Jana and Nicole, the best beta readers and friends a girl could ask for. Your kind words came when my writing confidence was at its lowest, and I always appreciate your love and support.

Thanks to my work, trivia, bowling, and theater people. Every time I feel unloved, I think of you and remember otherwise. Special shout-out to Matt and Jonny, proud supporters of the Year of Allee.

Thanks to Ryan, my daily reminder that beautiful things can come from honest conversations.

Thanks to my family. Your love and support mean everything to me. Special shout-out to Sam for answering all my alcohol and occupational therapy questions.

To my fellow aces and everyone else under the noncishet umbrella. You are loved, you are lovable, and your stories are worth telling.

ABOUT THE AUTHOR

Allee Mead is a writer from North Dakota. Her mom once bought her a pillow that says, "I just want to read books, pet dogs, & drink tea," which sums her up pretty well, actually. She has had some short stories and poems published in literary journals and appeared on one episode of Jeopardy! in June 2024. *Isaac* is her first novella.

Please take a moment to review this book at your favorite retailer's website, Goodreads, or simply tell your friends!